what

"Ever is very intriguing. It keeps your attention and makes it hard to put down. The descriptiveness reminds me of a John Grisham book, and I have read all of them. I would highly recommend Ever."

Charles Roberts
Tarkenton Financial

You are immediately transported into the action-packed and suspenseful story. It blends science fiction and the human element in a compelling way. A promising start by a young author.

Laura Sherman
Founding Partner Baldwin Krystyn Sherman Partners
& Baldwin Risk Partners

Ever is one of those books that leaves you asking "what's next!" The end of the chapters hook you to the next making you need more! The character Raya seems to be a girl who doesn't take no for an answer and is always looking for the next adventure. Ever is a great read!

Dr. Raul Serrano
Best-Selling Author
Ignite Chiropractic & Wellness

A tale of young love, friendship, and other dimensions, Ever will keep you at the edge of your seat in a captivating adventure with surprises at every turn. The author and her series is off to a thrilling start. Don't miss this!

Katie Griffith
Principal, Bright Solutions

KAYLEE STEPKOSKI
EVER

This is a work of fiction. Names, characters, and incidents are either a product of the author's imagination or are used fictitiously. Any resemblance to actual persons, living or dead, or events are entirely coincidental.

Copyright © 2019 Kaylee Stepkoski
All Rights Reserved. Printed in the U.S.A.
Published by Two Penny Publishing
850 E Lime Street #266, Tarpon Springs 34688

No part of this publication may be reproduced, distributed, or transmitted in any form or by any means, including photocopying, recording, or other electronic or mechanical methods, without the prior written permission of the publisher, except in the case of brief quotations embodied in critical reviews and certain other noncommercial uses permitted by copyright law.

For permission requests and ordering information, email the publisher at:
info.twopenny@gmail.com

Book Design by: Jodi Costa
Cover Photography by: Adrian Traurig
Cover Design by: Adrian Traurig

ISBN (book): 978-1-950995-00-4
ISBN (ebook): 978-1-950995-01-1

FIRST EDITION

For more information about Kaylee Stepkoski or to book her for your next event or media interview, please contact her representative at:
info.twopenny@gmail.com

table of contents

DEDICATION

chapter 1	THE SPACE MUSEUM	9
chapter 2	BLACK OUT	23
chapter 3	THE SIGNS	37
chapter 4	THE TRIP	49
chapter 5	THE BREAK IN	61
chapter 6	ANDREW	73
chapter 7	EVER	83
chapter 8	WAKE UP	93
chapter 9	PREPARATION	105
chapter 10	THE ESCAPE	113
chapter 11	PROBLEMS	125
chapter 12	QUESTIONS	137
chapter 13	DISCOVERIES	149
chapter 14	A NEW STRENGTH	165
chapter 15	CAUGHT	177
chapter 16	THE RISK	189
chapter 17	EVER'S METHOD	199
chapter 18	HER RETURN	211
chapter 19	GOODBYE	223
chapter 20	BELOVED	237

ACKNOWLEDGMENTS 247

dedication

This book is dedicated to my grandparents and great-grandparents, Daniel and Jane Sutton, Paul and Helen Stepkoski, Thomas and Imogene Bright, Daniel and Etrula Sutton, Casmir and Elizabeth Goscinski, and Stanley and Sophie Stepkoski. To you who immigrated to America from Poland, to you who served and fought in the Vietnam War and World War II, and to you who raised your children lovingly so future generations have every opportunity to be successful. Because of your love, sacrifice, and courage, I can follow my dreams. I love you and thank you with all my heart.

chapter one
THE SPACE MUSEUM

The last thing that I felt of Ever was the earth shake beneath me; then he was gone. It's amazing how something so close, but so far, can hurt so badly when it's gone.

My name is Raya Fawn. I live in Gail, Texas with my mom, Alivia. I've lived in Texas all my life, so about nineteen years. My father, Logan, died of cancer when I was nine, and now it's just my mom and me. I'm currently working on my Associates Degree online, so I'm home with my mom quite a bit. My mom and I have grown close since my dad's death, but she's also gone a lot going on business trips. My closest friend, Andrew, lives right down the street and is also working towards his degree online. We basically grew up together. Although, everything changed about six months ago, when I met Ever.

"Andrew! That's not funny! I'm not going to be homeless. I just need more time to figure out what I'm going to do with my life," I inform Andrew.

"Okay! I'm just making sure you're not acting lazy," Andrew responds with a smirk. Since my dad's passing, Andrew has always been by my side. He never fails to find a way to make me laugh and ease up on worrying.

"Whatever, when are we going to get there? I feel like you're driving extremely slow," I complain.

"We're almost there and chill; I'm not driving slow," Andrew replies.

Andrew and I are on our way to the Space Museum for a project we were assigned. I've always wanted to go to this museum because I feel like it's about the size of Texas.

As we pull up to the Space Museum, my jaw drops. I never knew how huge this place was. The sun is glimmering from behind the big museum's sign. I'm in awe with the many people walking in and out of this magnificent building. Then I feel the car stop, so I open the door. I stand by the side of the car door just staring at the building.

"Raya!" Andrew shouts.

"Huh?" I mutter.

"Hello? Are you seriously intrigued by this place? Besides this place being massive, I'm surprised that you're this interested," Andrew comments.

"Oh no! It's cool, I guess," I answer blushing.

"Mmhmm. Okay sure," Andrew says laughing. "Hey, why are there all of these military people here?" Andrew asks.

"Oh wow. I have no idea. I didn't see anything involving the military online," I reply in confusion.

Andrew made a good point. Why are there all of these military personnel here? I know this is a space museum, but is there something in there that needs protection or needs to be hidden? There are four military men patting down and searching every guest entering. I'm not sure if I should be afraid or excited.

Andrew and I walk up to the entrance. One of the guards asks to search my purse and another begins telling me how and where he's going to pat me down. Andrew looks at me confused, but I comply with what the guard says. We finally make it inside, and I'm stunned. The ceilings are monumentally high, and the building is so wide and long. Hundreds of people are shuffling in and out of the gift shops on the left side of the grand hallway and staring at many posters and photographs plastered up and down the right side. Among them are military personnel marching up and down the hallway. Out of the corner of my eye, I notice a line of formally dressed visitors blocked off by red ropes.

"Hey, what's that over there?" I ask Andrew.

"What, that line? Umm I don't know. Let's check it out,"

Andrew answers.

"Alright, let's do it," I add.

We walk up to the desk to the side of the line with a man standing there.

"Hey, sir. What is this?" Andrew asks the man standing at the desk.

"It's a limited time exhibit," the man clarifies.

"Oh, can my friend and I go in?" Andrew asks.

"Sure. Do you have a reservation?" the man asks.

"Reservation? Uh yeah," Andrew responds.

"Andrew!" I say under my breath.

"Shhh," Andrew mutters placing his hand on my shoulder, while standing up on his toes for a quick second to peer over the desk.

"Our reservation is under Bob Snyder, sir," Andrew informs confidently.

"Ah yes, Mr. Snyder. Come on in!" the man says with a smile.

"Thank you," Andrew replies politely. It's not surprising that he'd pull something like this. He always finds a way to make things happen.

Then Andrew and I stumble quickly to the back of the line.

"Andrew, are you crazy? We'll get in so much trouble!" I advise in a whisper.

"Oh hush. How will we get caught if the line is already filing into the exhibit?" Andrew asks with a wink.

I look up and see he's right. The line is moving fast into a door.

"Andrew…fine," I respond rolling my eyes, while trying to hide my smile of excitement.

We all enter this fairly large, square, poorly lit, empty room, and a soldier begins giving us directions as we cluster around him.

"Attention! You have all entered a secure location. There will be no photos or videos permitted. Each party will enter the exhibit momentarily, but please stay between the red velvet curtains. Do not go behind them! Thank you for your patience," the soldier informs us sharply.

"Andrew, I'm embarrassed to say this, but I'm nervous. What did we get ourselves into?" I ask Andrew as I turn white.

"We're going to be fine. This will be fun, trust me," Andrew assures as he puts his arm around me and rubs my arm.

Like the soldier said, each attending party enters the exhibit room in their own time. Oddly, each party that goes into the exhibit is inside for different amounts of time. The first party was in there for about five minutes, but the second party was in there for less than two minutes. I stand in fear. I start thinking to myself, *Should I be afraid? Maybe not.*

"Last group!" the soldier announces.

Andrew and I begin to enter the exhibit room. It's strange. There are red velvet curtains that are maybe seven feet tall that form a tight walkway. The beaming ceiling lights make the walkway bright, but everything else is dark.

"Andrew, will you go in front of me?" I ask nervously.

"Sure," Andrew replies with a slight chuckle.

Thankfully, Andrew starts first, then I follow. It may seem silly to ask Andrew to go before me, because I'm anxious, but ever since my dad passed, my anxiety level has risen. My dad was always my rock providing encouragement and motivation whenever I needed it, but now he's gone. So now when my nerves are on edge, I become flustered and overwhelmed. Andrew knows that I struggle with this, so he's done his best in being my support.

As I enter the long walkway, I feel the cool air touch my skin. The velvet curtains brush across my hands as I nervously begin walking down the aisle. I start to squint as the lights shine down on me. *What is this place? What's going to happen?*

The walkway begins to widen out, forming a small room which is still enclosed by the velvet curtains. Andrew and I walk into the small room, where there is a formally dressed soldier and a tall, slightly transparent, thin, strong man. He looks my age. He has dark blue eyes and short, dark blonde hair. I glance up at Andrew with a confused expression. Then he looks at me and notices my confusion.

"I think the tall dude is the exhibit," Andrew whispers in my ear.

"Oh. Hmm," I respond a little more confused.

The tall man locks eyes with mine. I suddenly feel my insides rumble like an earthquake. I inhale quickly, trying to catch my breath as my lungs shake. Andrew sees me struggling to breathe as I continue to stare into the man's wide eyes. Andrew grabs my hand immediately, which makes me look away from the man. The rumbling suddenly stops, and I finally catch my breath. Andrew has a very concerned look on his face.

"You okay?" Andrew asks me in a slight panic.

"Yeah, I'm fine," I answer trying to calm myself down as I pull my hand out of his.

It's quiet for what feels like an eternity, until I break the silence.

"Hello. Who or what are you?" I ask the transparent man.

I suddenly realize I just asked the man a peculiar question, but the formally dressed soldier answers before him.

"He's alien," the soldier replies.

"Alien, as in he is an alien or he…"

"Classified," the soldier snaps cutting me off.

"Okay," I mutter softly.

I see the strange man try to lock eyes with me again, but I make no attempt to lock eyes with his.

"What's your name?" I ask the alien man.

"Ever," the strange man replies with his deep voice.

"Ever," I repeat. "I like that name."

I see a smile snap on and quickly off of Ever's face.

"How old are you?" Andrew quickly asks.

"I am 546 years old, or 19 in human reality," Ever replies.

Andrew and I both turn white with fear and curiosity. Physically, Ever appears 19, like me, but he's in fact 546. That's strange. I guess to him years are interpreted differently, similar to how dog years work.

"Where are you from?" I ask Ever.

"I can show you," Ever responds as he gestures to the curtains to his right.

The soldier stops him and begins whispering something to Ever. The only thing I can hear is "that's classified." Ever obeys and stands still. Then something strange begins to occur. Ever's body starts to blip into nothing then back to his transparent state very rapidly. Andrew and I gasp.

"I can hear them again! I can see them again!" Ever moans to the soldier, as he winces in pain.

Then everything begins to shake: the room, the curtains, the floors, and the building. The soldier has a worried expression on his face. Andrew wraps his arms around me, trying to shield me from falling ceiling tiles.

"Ever!" I scream over the shaking. "Look at me!"

Ever looks up at me and seems to relax. Then everything stops shaking, and Ever returns to his normal transparency. Then Andrew lets go of me while remaining alert.

"Are you guys okay?" the formally dressed soldier asks.

"You alright?" Andrew whispers to me.

"Yes," I reply still shaking.

"Yeah, we're fine," Andrew responds sharply to the soldier.

"You have a few more minutes left," the soldier informs.

There is complete silence again, until…

"What is your name?" Ever asks.

"Me?" I ask.

Ever nods.

"My name's Raya," I reply nervously.

"Raya," Ever repeats in his deep voice. "I like that."

"Thanks," I say while blushing with a smile.

Ever begins to smile, but it quickly disappears when Andrew begins to speak.

"Alright, thanks for letting us visit," Andrew says quickly.

"Yeah, thank you," I add while first looking at Ever, then to the soldier.

The soldier nods then pulls a curtain to the side, which reveals the exit. Andrew starts walking towards the exit, while beginning to grab my hand. Although, I pull away a little.

"Bye, Ever," I say.

"Goodbye, Raya," Ever replies with a soft grin.

Andrew pulls me out of the exhibit room; we walk back out into the huge museum. Then Andrew stares at me with a concerned and angry look.

"What?" I ask a little confused.

"What were you doing in there, Raya?" Andrew asks rather loudly.

"What do you mean?" I ask even more confused.

"Raya, you were in a dangerous situation, and you were flirting with that strange guy," Andrew replies with annoyance.

"I was not flirting! I was trying to help!" I argue angrily.

"Raya! You were flirting! And you shouldn't have tried to help because you could have been hurt," Andrew informs with a concerned look.

I pause. Andrew was making a valid point. I was trying to help a 546-year-old man. Then I kind of flirted–with Ever. I begin to blush.

"I'm sorry. You're right. I was acting childish–thank you for protecting me though. You saved me from multiple ceiling tiles," I respond while still blushing.

"Raya, it's fine. I'm just glad you're okay," Andrew says while patting my shoulder.

We continue to walk through the crowded hallway of

the Space Museum, but we're both silent. I notice dust on the floor and a few scared kids in one of the gift shops. Ever caused a lot of damage, but how? And what did Ever mean by, "I hear them again, and I see them again?" What did that soldier mean by "alien?" Did he really mean that? Eventually, Andrew and I decide to leave, so we head towards the museum's exit.

"What's this?" Andrew asks in surprise.

"What?" I ask while looking.

Everyone exiting the museum stops to sign something. When we reach the exit, a guard tells us to sign our name and address on a sheet of paper. Andrew asks why, but the only answer he gets is "security purposes," so we do what we're told. We finally make it out of the museum and get back to Andrew's car. During most of the car ride home, we're silent.

"That was weird," I comment, breaking the silence.

"What's weird?" Andrew asks.

"What happened at the museum, with Ever," I clarify.

"Yeah, that was," Andrew says, seriously, but then he begins to laugh.

"Why are you laughing?" I ask, feeling a little annoyed.

"Raya, you were flirting with an alien man!" Andrew announces laughing even louder.

"Shut up!" I yell while smiling and covering my face with my hands.

"Ha! Relax, I'm joking!" Andrew says with a smirk look.

"Ugh!" I groan.

We pull up into my driveway.

"Alright. Home sweet home," Andrew states.

"Thanks for the ride, and thank you for shielding me," I say with a smile.

"Anytime!" Andrew replies with a grin.

Andrew waves as I walk up to my deck. Once he drives away, I open the front door and walk inside.

"Mom, I'm home!" I announce.

"Hey, I'm in the kitchen! How was the museum?" my mom asks.

"Fine. It was pretty crowded." I reply as I find her in the kitchen.

I place my purse on the counter and open the refrigerator looking for a snack.

"Why is there dust on your shoulder, Raya?" my mom asks with a giggle.

"Oh! Umm maybe from Andrew's car," I reply, with a nervous smile.

"Ah, probably," my mom says with a laugh.

I eat my snack, then I head upstairs, where I sit down on my bed trying to process everything that had happened today and Ever. I cannot get Ever out of my mind. What was he? And how did he shake everything–even my insides? I have to know, but I can never get back into that exhibit again without a reservation. Even if I tried, it's a limited time exhibit, which means it's probably all booked. I shrug hoping that sleeping on it may help.

* EVER *

chapter two

BLACKOUT

Shaking, shaking, shaking, and sounds of rumbling. Many falling objects crashing on the ground and on me.

"Andrew!" I yell.

Crashing. Sharp pains spiking in my body.

"What's going on?!" I yell even louder.

"Raya!" anonymously announced in a deep voice. "Raya?!

"Who's–huh–Ever!!" I scream out. "Ever!"

I feel like I'm being swallowed by darkness. I can't breathe! Then I gasp, and I spring from my bed, panting.

"It was just a dream," I assure myself.

I lay down and fall back to sleep again.

Last night was a long night. I couldn't stop thinking about Ever and how Andrew risked himself to protect me. I don't know what to think. Maybe I should call Andrew. No, he'll just make fun of me, maybe; I don't know. I should just finish my assignment. I walk over to my desk and get started.

The next day comes, and I still don't know what to make of the other day. Still contemplating, I go downstairs to get some breakfast.

"Mom?" I shout.

No answer. I think she left for work. She'll probably be home around 6:30 tonight. Suddenly I hear knocking on the door, so I run over to answer.

"Hello?" I ask, as I answer the door.

"Hey, what's up?" Andrew asks with a smile.

"Oh hey! My mom's not home, so let me freshen up, and I'll come outside," I reply quickly.

"Okay, I'll be out here," Andrew says.

I quickly run upstairs and freshen up. Then I run back downstairs and go outside to find Andrew.

"Hey, sorry, I'm back," I tell Andrew out of breath.

"You're fine," Andrew responds. "Are you okay? The other day was just crazy, and I'm still a little rattled too."

"I'm alright. I've been having some strange dreams about what happened, and I can't get Ever out of my head," I explain.

"Yeah, I'm having the same problems," Andrew adds shrugging.

Andrew and I sit on the deck trying to process everything that happened at the museum.

We both are stumped about Ever. None of what happened made any sense.

Without warning, the deck under us begins to shake. Then the trees begin to shiver like the earth beneath them. Random sprinklers in my yard and neighboring yards go off, and power lines begin to shatter with sparks flying into the streets. All I hear is rumbling and my heart pounding. I look at Andrew, and he looks as terrified as I am. We're stuck sitting in deck chairs, paralyzed with fear. Then it stops; everything stops shaking. Leaves fall onto my head from the shaken trees.

"What the heck was that?" Andrew asks with a shiver in his voice.

I'm still trying to collect myself from what just occurred.

"I–uh–don't–know," I finally reply with a shaky voice.

Abruptly, loud sirens begin going off all around us. I then hear helicopters with their whipping propellers from above. I look up to see where they are, and I discover one. It's green–the military? I glance to Andrew to alert him, but he's staring at the dozens of military vehicles pulling up to my house. Many soldiers jump out of the vehicles and come running up my yard with large guns. Andrew jumps up and grabs my arm, then he pulls me up and out of my paralyzed state.

"Raya Fawn!" one of the soldiers calls out, running up to the deck stairs.

I'm frozen and unable to comprehend what's going on. My face feels scorching hot with fear, but my hands and feet feel ice cold. I look to Andrew for support, but he's as frozen as I am. I feel his fearful hand squeezing my arm, still and unable to relax.

"Yes?" I finally manage to blurt out.

"We need you to come with us now!" the soldier announces.

"No way! She's not going with you guys!" Andrew snaps back, as he finally releases my arm and clenches his fists.

"We're not asking—it's an order!" the soldier demands, right back to Andrew.

"Andrew, it's okay," I say. "I'll come, but Andrew has to come too."

"Fine," the soldier grunts.

The soldiers come up the deck steps and lead Andrew and me to one of the military vehicles. Although, when we reach the vehicle, the soldiers don't load us in. They place our hands on the side of the truck, while they pat us down. Finally, when they finish, one of the helicopters lands in the street and the soldiers lead us there. My long, brown hair snaps my cheeks and ears from the violent winds caused by the propellers of the helicopter, and my clothes whip in every direction. When we reach the helicopter, the soldiers load us inside and strap us in. Then they fasten headsets on our heads.

I'm looking everywhere frantically trying to collect myself, but it's impossible.

"So, are you statues going to tell us where we're going and why?" Andrew asks the soldiers with an attitude.

"To the Space Museum," a soldier answers.

"Ever?" I ask under my breath.

Then I peer out the side of the helicopter and glance down. I notice water pouring out of pipelines in the streets and cracks along roads. I also see fallen trees and firetrucks racing to houses. All of this damage is tragic to see. Then I remember my mom! Is she okay? She has no idea where I am! I remember she won't be back home until about 6:30 tonight. What time is it now?

"Hey, Andrew. Do you know what time it is?" I ask.

"Uh, I don't know," Andrew replies.

A soldier sitting next to Andrew must have heard me through the headset. The soldier waves at me and gets my attention.

"It's 13:00," the soldier informs me.

"What?" I mouth to myself.

Andrew notices me struggling to understand.

"The soldier means it's 1:00 pm," Andrew explains to me.

"Oh okay," I reply. I have at least five and a half hours until my mom gets home. I think that's enough time.

The helicopter begins its descent. When it lands, the

soldiers unstrap us and unload us from the helicopter. Then I stare at the magnificent Space Museum, and my jaw drops. The once grand building is covered in cracks and holes, and a corner of the building had slid right off. My eyes begin to fill with tears, but I quickly pull them back as the soldiers lead us to the building. Finally, we reach the front of the shattered museum, and I feel sharp chills go up my spine.

"Raya!" announces from inside the museum. "Raya!"

"It's Ever!" I shout. "Where is he?"

Andrew glares at me with anger and fear.

"He's inside and he's flickering in and out of his transparent state again," a soldier answers. "How did you make him stop?"

"I–uh–I don't know," I reply nervously.

Another soldier leads Andrew and me inside. Shattered glass, dust, and pieces of wall and ceiling are scattered everywhere across the floor. Then the soldier brings us through the exhibit doors and the now half-hung, red velvet curtains. We reach the small room where Ever is located. I see him hunched over, yelling in pain.

"Raya! Ughh I hear them, and they will not stop! Aghh I see them...everywhere!" Ever yells, as he clenches the sides of his head with his hands.

"Ever!" I shout back.

No answer. Andrew moves closer to me, on high alert. The room starts to shake. Ceiling tiles begin falling. Andrew wraps his arms around me again and shields me from the tiles. I try again.

"Ever!" I scream. "Ever, I'm right here!"

No answer again, and Ever groans louder. The room and building shake even more. I know what I have to do. I push away Andrew's arms and run toward Ever. My feet are buzzing from the shaking floor beneath me, but I try for a third time.

"Ever!" I scream again.

The soldiers begin scrambling towards Andrew and me to get us out of the crumbling building. I can't let them take me yet; I have to help Ever, so I reach my hand out towards Ever's clenching arm.

"Ever!" I scream again, as I place my left hand on his arm.

As I touch Ever's arm, I feel the sensation of sharp, burning needles running up my arm, then my entire body. He looks up at me. He doesn't return to his normal transparency; he is not transparent at all. His eyes flash from a glittering white to a dark blue. I lock my green eyes on his and his lock on mine. The earth below my feet stops shaking, but now my insides are shaking. My hand on Ever's arm begins to vibrate and so does the rest of my body. Although, I can't unlock my eyes from his.

"Raya! Your arm!" Andrew yells behind me.

I look at my left arm. It has glowing white, alien-like

signs embedded in my skin from my fingertips to my elbow. I pull my hand back from Ever's arm. He returns to his normal transparency. My arm stops glowing, but I continue to shake. The shaking inside of me gets harder and harder until, snap! My body whips with a snap-like sound and motion to the floor. My eyes are blurry, and my body is heavy and as still as stone. I watch Andrew jump to my side and grab my face. He sounds muffled; I think he's telling me to keep my eyes open. Then I roll my head towards Ever's direction. I see him looking down at me with a shocked and terrified look. He begins to bend down towards me, maybe trying to help, but four of the soldiers shove him away with their guns. I try to say Ever's name, but nothing comes out. Then Andrew rolls my face back towards his. He's trying to tell me something, but I can't hear him, or anything now. Everything fades into darkness; everything's black.

I feel cool, relaxed, and numb. Then I feel a warm, familiar hand clenching mine. I slowly open my heavy eyes, and I look up, but it's still a little blurry. There are bright white lights shining down on me. I see blue blankets on top of me, and I hear a faded familiar voice.

"Raya. You're okay. You're in the hospital," Andrew says in a muffled voice.

"The hospital? What—why?" I try to ask, but my mouth feels heavy.

"Raya, Ever really injured you, so the military flew you to the closest hospital," Andrew replies in a quiet voice.

"Injured? I—I feel okay," I say softly, trying to keep my eyes open.

"You have major bruises from your neck down to your tail bone," Andrew responds.

"Bruises?" I mumble. "From Ever?"

"Yeah," Andrew answers, now holding my hand with both of his.

I begin to smile when I see him holding my hand, but then a doctor walks in.

"Ah Raya Fawn, you're awake! You may feel drowsy from the pain killers we gave you," the doctor informs.

"Pain killers? There's bruising…" I try to say.

"Raya, you have suffered a great amount of trauma to your spine. Thankfully, the x-rays show that you have no broken bones, but you'll have a lot of pain in that area for the next few weeks," the doctor explains.

"Weeks?" I finally ask clearly.

"This was a major amount of trauma, Raya. I wish I could give you a more accurate recovery time, but your bodyguards won't give any specifics as to what happened," the doctor says, with a bit of frustration in his voice.

"Bodyguards?" I ask Andrew.

"The military sent a few soldiers to watch out for us,"

Andrew replies.

"Oh okay," I respond. "Umm, when can I leave?"

"Raya," Andrew tries to say.

"I will discharge you in a few hours since all you need is medication and rest," the doctor answers.

"Okay, thank you," I say to the doctor.

"Alright, let me know if you need anything, Raya," the doctor mentions with a smile as he leaves the room.

"Thanks," Andrew says to the doctor.

Andrew looks at me with a smile. Then I turn my head, and I notice a clock on the wall.

"It's 4:00!" I shout in a panic.

"Shhh! You still have two and a half hours until your mom gets home, so you're fine," Andrew reassures.

"Fine? How is she not going to find out? Andrew, I'm in a hospital bed!" I yell louder.

"Raya, the military took care of all of it since you were injured under their watch," Andrew explains, trying to calm me down.

"All of it? No records? No bills?" I repeat. "Okay, I feel a little better now."

"Good," Andrew says with a chuckle.

Then I try to sit up, but I can't seem to find enough strength in my arms. Suddenly Andrew sees my attempt to get up.

"Whoa, careful," Andrew advises, trying to help me.

Andrew puts his hands under my arms and raises me up. He sits me up against a pillow, where he lets me down gently. Then he sits back down.

"Better?" Andrew asks.

"Yeah, thank you," I answer with a smile. "Andrew, what happened to Ever?" I ask.

Andrew's face becomes hard. His knuckles turn white as he squeezes his hands tightly in his lap.

"Andrew," I state firmly.

"Uhh—after you blacked out, a few soldiers shoved him away. I didn't see him again until you were loaded into the helicopter. He was put into some big military truck, then the truck drove off," Andrew explains.

"Poor Ever," I say quietly.

"Poor Ever?" Andrew yells. "Raya, you could have died! Ever did this to you and look at you! You can barely move!" Andrew exclaims.

"Andrew, I…" I try to say, but I'm cut off.

"No, Raya! This is ridiculous," Andrew grumbles, as he walks out of the room.

I sit alone, not really sure why Andrew's so upset. Then, I look to the window and I see some cracks in the glass–maybe from Ever. I pull my legs to the edge of the bed. I try to lift myself off the bed, but my arms keep giving out.

Finally, on the third try, I get up. I wobble a little on the cold hospital floor, but I adjust my footing. Then I look over my right shoulder, and I see a mirror on the wall behind me. My hospital smock is slightly open. I pull my smock, so the opening widens. Now, I see my whole back. From my neck all the way down to my lower back, there's a huge, black, blue, and purple bruise. I gasp, and my eyes fill with tears. Then a tear escapes my eye and slides down my cheek.

"Everything's going to be fine," I say in a shaky voice, trying to reassure myself.

I close my smock and wobble over to the window. I look at the sky, trying to get my mind off things. Then Andrew walks in.

"Raya? What are you doing up?" Andrew asks in a panic.

"I wanted to move around," I reply, as he walks me back to the bed.

"Hey, I'm sorry for getting upset. I'm just stressed and overwhelmed with what happened with you and Ever," Andrew explains.

"It's okay, Andrew. I was being ridiculous," I add.

We're both silent for a few minutes. Then the doctor walks in.

"Alright, you've been discharged. I'm sure you need a wheelchair, right?" the doctor asks.

I was about to say, no.

"Yes," Andrew replies over me.

Andrew and the doctor help me into the wheelchair. Then one of the soldiers rolls me out, while Andrew follows. A military truck outside of the hospital drives us home. It's around 6:25 when we arrive at Andrew's house.

"You going to be okay?" Andrew asks me when he jumps out.

"Yeah," I reply.

"Call me if you need anything," Andrew says, as he backs away from the truck.

I nod. Then the truck drives away from his house and pulls into my driveway at 6:30. A soldier helps me stand up out of the truck, then they drive off. I hobble to the front door and open it.

"Mom!" I announce, hoping for no answer.

No answer.

"Yes!" I say to myself, thinking that she will not uncover what happened today.

I shuffle into the kitchen to grab a snack, then I go to my room upstairs. I hide my medication under my bed, when I hear car brakes outside.

"Raya!" my mom announces, as she walks inside the house.

"Hey!" I say, as I grab my laptop and sit on my bed.

I hear my mom come upstairs. So, I quickly set the

laptop on my lap and gently lay my back on a pillow against the headboard of my bed. My assignment pulls up as soon as she walks into my room.

"Did you feel that earthquake?" my mom asks in disbelief.

"Earthquake? Yeah, I felt a little rumble," I respond hesitantly.

My mom giggles.

"Well, what else did you do today?" my mom asks.

"Well, when it rumbled, I did fall–onto the floor. Now, I'm working on my assignment," I reply nervously.

"Oh, I'm sorry. Are you okay?" my mom asks.

"Yeah, I'm fine!" I respond, trying to add a little enthusiasm.

"Okay. Well, I'm going to my room because I'm exhausted; work was hectic from the earthquake," my mom informs me.

"Yeah, I'm going to bed also. Today was pretty hectic," I say as she walks off.

I put my laptop on my nightstand and lay down. Then I feel a sharp pain spike up and down my back, so I roll over to my side. That helps some with the pain. I slowly close my eyes. My head gets light, and I feel my body relax. A few minutes pass, and I finally fall asleep.

chapter three

THE SIGNS

Darkness overwhelms my sight. It's pitch black, but I can see my hands when I look at them, like I'm the only thing visible. I try to walk, but I feel no pressure on my feet. Then I look to my hands again, to try and comprehend what's happening. I gasp. My left hand is glowing with white alien-like signs embedded in my skin, from the tips of my fingers to my elbow—just like at the museum. I touch my glowing forearm with my other hand, and I feel a tingling warmth on my fingertips coming from my forearm. Then I hear something. Quiet breathing, maybe. My eyes begin searching around me, but there's nothing. It's just complete darkness.

"Raya," an anonymous whisper says.

"Huh?" I try to find words.

I begin to feel a deep chill go down my spine in fear.

"Hello? Who's there? What's on my arm? What's going on?" I start blurting out.

I start to shake in fear as I look around, but there's nothing. Nothing at all, just black. Then I finally find something, no, *someone*.

"Ever?" I ask in a shaky voice.

My vision begins to sharpen, and I now see Ever in his transparent self; although, he looks far away. I try walking to him slowly, but I can't tell if I'm moving at all. Then I peer to him in frustration and confusion. He sees my frustration, and he suddenly flickers from far away to a few feet in front of me.

"What's going on?" I ask him in shock.

"You are in a vision that I have created," Ever answers.

"A vision? H–how?" I ask with hesitation.

"When you touched my arm, I felt a part of me cross over to you. You must have absorbed something, but I cannot figure out how–especially your kind," Ever explains with a confused expression.

"My kind? Absorbed? Wait, hold on! What are you talking about?" I shriek with fear.

"Raya, you are okay. I cannot explain the absorption part, because I have never seen someone of your kind absorb like that," Ever replies warmly.

"Once again, what do you mean by your kind?" I yell.

"Raya, you and I are different. You are made of mostly

water, but I am made up of a–foreign substance," Ever explains hesitantly.

"Foreign?" I blurt out.

Ever's dark blue eyes flicker around. Maybe with uncertainty or fear.

"Ever, you have to give me some answers," I implore in frustration.

"Raya, I am not human. I am from Earth like you, but not the Earth you are familiar with. And the figures on your arm–they are similar to small transmitters. I can feel what you feel. What you feel emotionally and what you feel physically," Ever explains.

I don't know what to think or what to say. I can't wrap my head around what Ever just said.

"Raya, I am sorry for the pain I put you through. I constantly feel the excruciating pain you experience in the back of my mind. When you fell, I immediately felt what you were feeling. I tried to help, but I was taken away," Ever says with a concerned look.

Suddenly Ever begins to flicker in and out of his transparent state and into nothing.

"Wait, Ever!" I shout.

"Raya, I will try to communicate with you again, but I am out of time," Ever informs in his deep, warm voice.

Ever has a small grin on his face, then he disappears. I'm

alone again in a black abyss.

"Raya!" someone shouts. "Hello? Raya!" someone shouts again.

My eyes unlock from a deep sleep, and I begin to breathe heavily with fear.

"Raya! Girl, you need to get up!" my mom announces, as she walks into my room.

"Oh sorry," I respond in a groggy voice.

"You look exhausted, Raya. Did you sleep okay?" my mom asks.

"Umm yeah. I was just having some weird dreams about the earthquake," I explain nervously.

"Ah, okay. Well, I'm going to work, so I'll see you when I get back. Love you!" mom announces as she leaves my room.

"Love you too," I reply in a sleepy voice.

As she leaves I remember that I need to take my medication, so I need to get up. I begin to try and sit up, but the pain running up and down my back stops me. I lay back down again trying to hold back my tears. I try rolling over. Now, I'm on my stomach, and I slide off my bed. Finally, I am able to reach under my bed and take my medication. Then I use my desk chair to lift myself off the floor.

Eventually, I make it downstairs and grab a vanilla yogurt from the refrigerator. I open the container and begin to stir the white, thick liquid. I investigate it carefully, and I notice all of the white swirls I've made. Suddenly, I remember my vision of the white signs in my arm. I stare at where the signs were, and I don't see them, so I wonder if the vision was even real. It felt real; I know it was real…was it?

A week has passed. I haven't seen Andrew since that terrifying day at the museum. He's called a few times, but I didn't have the guts to answer until yesterday. I still don't know what to say to him; he saved my life. After his persistence, I agreed to let him come over later today, and I'm kind of nervous. Luckily, my back feels a little better. I can walk normally, but it's still very painful to bend over.

I'm expecting Andrew to arrive any minute, so I'm all freshened up. Since it's the weekend, my mom will be home, and it'll be difficult to talk to Andrew without her overhearing.

"Raya, Andrew's at the door!" my mom announces as she's about to open the door.

"Hi, Mrs. Fawn," Andrew greets.

"Hey, Andrew. Raya will be down in a minute," my mom says.

I quickly hobble downstairs to meet Andrew at the door.

"Hey, Andrew. You want to hang out on the front deck?" I ask.

"Yeah," Andrew replies.

Andrew and I walk out onto the deck. He sits down in the deck chair, and I begin to sit down as well.

"Ahh," I mumble as I sit down.

"Well, I'm guessing you're not feeling much better," Andrew states with a concerned look.

"What? No, I'm fine," I reply.

"Yeah, sure. Well, anyway, how have you been since, you know, the museum?" Andrew asks.

"That was a crazy day. I'm still having nightmares," I answer, trying to get comfortable in the deck chair.

"Same here. Mostly because your arm started to glow, and the snapping sound your body made is all I hear," Andrew explains with a terrified expression.

My mind suddenly flies back to that moment. I have a slight memory of that snap, but all I really remember was being afraid.

Suddenly my mom runs out the front door and to her car.

"Mom, you okay?" I shout to her as I sit up in the deck chair.

"Not really! Something happened at work with one of my accounts, and they need me immediately," my mom answers, as she starts her car and drives off.

"Hmm weird," I mutter, as I start to lean back again.

I suddenly feel a terrible sharp pain shoot up my back.

"Ahh," I groan.

"Raya, I'm so sorry. This was all my fault. I never should've let you get near Ever," Andrew says.

"Ever needed help! That was my choice, not yours," I explain.

"I should have stopped you, though. Then you never would've been injured," Andrew adds with a disappointed look.

"You wouldn't have been able to stop me. I needed to help Ever," I reply while rubbing where the signs were in my arm.

"Oh, I meant to ask this. Uh, do you have any idea why those symbol things showed up in that arm?" Andrew asks, while pointing to the arm I was rubbing.

"No," I answer immediately.

"Well, hopefully those things don't show up again," Andrew says with a nod.

"Yeah," I respond a little hesitantly.

Andrew looks up at me quizzically.

"Why'd you say it like that?" Andrew asks.

"Like what?" I ask trying to cover my bluff.

"You hesitated. They showed up again, didn't they?" Andrew shouts, as he springs from the deck chair.

"Uhh no!" I plead.

"Raya! I know you're hiding something. When did they show up again?" Andrew asks as he grabs my arm to inspect it.

"They didn't exactly show up like you would think," I reply.

"What do you mean?" Andrew asks after he lets go of my arm.

"They showed up in a dream or vision I had last night. I felt my arm, and the embedded signs were warm and tingly. I saw Ever too. He was telling me that he wasn't from the Earth I know, and he wasn't human like me. He also told me that when I touched his arm, I drew something out of him. That's why my arm glows. The glowing signs are like transmitters, so he can feel what I feel physically and emotionally," I explain.

Andrew slowly sits back down in the deck chair again. His face looks shocked and terrified at the same time.

"Andrew?" I ask.

"Raya, you're telling me that he transmits your feelings, or whatever, constantly? And you absorbed that from him?" Andrew asks a bit loudly.

"I'm not very sure. I think only when the signs show up and glow," I say, trying to wrap my head around everything.

"You know, all of that may have been just a dream," Andrew states taking a deep breath.

"That's what I'm trying to tell myself, but Ever told me he made the vision," I explain nervously.

"A vision? Okay Raya, you're really freaking me out," Andrew says, folding his hands tightly in his lap.

"How do you think I feel?" I ask trying to smile.

Andrew begins to relax his hands and looks up at me. He

grins a little, but he still looks worried.

"Will those signs in your arm go away?" Andrew asks.

"I honestly have no idea," I reply shrugging. "Maybe Ever can fix it."

"Ever? No way!" Andrew shouts.

"Andrew," I sigh.

"No! I never want to see that freak again," Andrew informs angrily.

"I know you don't, but he can probably help me," I advise.

"Raya, even if he could help you, Ever is probably in some hidden military base, and I would never let you go near him," Andrew says strictly.

"Andrew, Ever doesn't want to hurt me, and stop being so dramatic," I add trying to ignore him.

Andrew stands up and begins pacing back and forth on the deck. Andrew's right. How am I going to find Ever? There are probably only a few military personnel that know exactly where Ever is located. And why would any of them tell a teenager where he is?

Andrew finally stops pacing and is leaning up against the deck railing. I can tell he's frustrated but also trying to see my point. Suddenly I hear thunder, but not from the sky, from the ground! The earth shakes under us with crackling and crashing thunder. Andrew looks at me to see if I've noticed. He stumbles over to me and helps me out of the trembling deck chair. The trees begin shivering, causing leaves to flutter all around us. Andrew gently, but quickly, lifts me out of the deck chair. He carries me into the front yard and stands me up. We watch everything shake. We're too terrified to say anything, so we stand like statues as the earth shakes under us.

"Ahh!" I scream as I fall to the ground.

"Raya!" Andrew yells as he crouches to the ground to help me.

I'm on the ground in excruciating pain. It feels like thousands of needles and knives are stabbing all over my body. I manage to look around to see why I'm in so much pain. Then I notice my arm is glowing again with the embedded alien signs.

"Agh!" I scream even louder.

Andrew sees my left arm glowing with signs. He put his hands on his head as he tries to figure out what to do. The piercing needles and knives are joined with an intense burning sensation. The pain is overwhelming me, and my vision starts to become dark. Andrew sees me slipping away into unconsciousness. He tries sitting me up and tells me something, but I can't hear him over the thundering earth below us. Before my vision goes completely dark, I remember that Ever feels my emotions. Maybe he can sense what the emotions are caused by, the pain, like they are connected.

"Ever," I whisper.

The shaking slowly begins to stop, but my arm continues to glow.

"Ever," I state in a louder whisper. "Stop, you're hurting me."

The shaking stops, and my arm suddenly begins to dim. The signs sink away and disappear. My hearing comes back again, and my vision clears up.

"Raya! Raya, look at me! Are you okay?" Andrew shouts while still sitting me up.

"Andrew," I groan.

Andrew lifts me up and carries me back into the house. He gently lays me down on the living room couch and sits on a stool next to me.

"Andrew?" I whisper.

"Raya, your arm isn't glowing anymore, but do you still feel pain?" Andrew asks.

"No, thankfully," I reply with a small grin.

"You think that was Ever?" Andrew asks.

"Yes, and I think I figured it out too," I answer.

"Figured what out? The glowing?" Andrew asks with an interested and worried look.

"Yeah. I think Ever and I can feel each other's emotions and physical sensations when my arm glows. Like our feelings are in sync or something. I called out his name, and I think he felt that, so he calmed down, but not entirely. When I called out his name again, I think he realized what was happening and subsided the shaking and thundering," I explain in a serious tone.

"That sounds like a possible explanation," Andrew says.

I glance at Andrew, and he's staring deeply at my arm. Then he locks his eyes on mine.

"We need to find Ever," Andrew informs with an intense look.

chapter four

THE TRIP

A few days pass, as Andrew endlessly searches online to find any possible military base in Texas. There has been some shaking here and there, and my arm would glow, but Ever would eventually make it stop. Andrew is freaking out, so he keeps checking on me. Sadly, there has been no luck in finding Ever. Andrew has looked everywhere, and Ever hasn't appeared in my dreams in a while. We feel stuck. How are we going to find him? We need to free him, and I need him to help me. I don't know if Andrew and I are going to find him.

When my mom returned, after she left in a hurry a few days ago, I asked her about what happened, and she told me that she almost lost an important account in the company, but thankfully she convinced them to stay. Also, Andrew and I have put aside our assignment for now to focus on searching for bases in Texas, and still no luck. It was another long day, so I decided to go to bed early. As soon as I close my eyes, I'm in a deep sleep. I'm in complete black again. Another vision maybe? I frantically look around to see if I can find Ever. Nothing.

"Ever!" I shout.

"Raya," I hear in return.

Suddenly Ever appears right in front of me.

"Ever, why haven't you spoken to me? It's been days!" I inform.

"Raya, I am sorry. I have been unable to communicate, because I am never alone here. There are too many guards, and I do not want them to find out that I am connecting with you," Ever explains.

"Ever, tell me where you are! I can help you, and you need to help me," I reveal.

"What is wrong?" Ever asks with a concerned look.

I lift my arm and show it to him, revealing the glowing, white, alien signs. Ever reaches out and holds my arm in his hands. After he looks at the glowing, embedded signs, he looks at me.

"Ever–I don't think you understand how painful this is. I can't bare the pain anymore. It's too much," I say while beginning to tear up.

Ever has a shocked look on his face. Then he rubs his

fingers from my elbow to my fingers. I feel a brief cooling sensation on my arm where he rubs, but as soon as he lets go, the burning needles come back.

"Raya, I had no idea it has been hurting you," Ever says in a hesitant voice.

"Ever, you said you can feel my pain. I can also feel yours, when my arm glows," I reply with an annoyed expression.

"You can feel mine?" Ever whispers with a grimace.

"Uhh yeah. You didn't know?" I ask with a confused look.

"Oh no. I need to find you, now," Ever advises with a hard expression.

"What? Am I okay?" I ask nervously.

"You appear fine for now, but I need to find you," Ever informs.

I feel stunned and cold with fear. Why is Ever so concerned? Should I be?

"Ever, you're never going to be able to get out of a military base. Tell me where you are! I can find you," I say quickly.

Ever begins to pace a little, while also squeezing his fists. I notice the veins in his hands beginning to glow in white.

"Ever?" I ask in a shaky voice.

"They are holding me at the NAS Corpus Christi Naval Base, but I am not in the base. They custom-made a cell for me in the water," Ever finally says.

"In the water?" I ask in disbelief.

Ever's quiet. I'm not sure if I should be terrified, but I am.

"Raya, I need to go, and I will see you when you arrive. In the meantime, remember this: do not let anyone touch your arm if it glows again," Ever informs strictly.

Then he suddenly disappears. I'm alone again, and I don't know what to think. Why was Ever so… fearful?

My eyes slowly begin to open. I look around my room, as sunrays beam through my curtains. I roll out of bed, and my back aches a little, but I'm able to get up. Then I walk over to my desk and open my laptop, where I type NAS Corpus Christi Naval Base into my search engine. I find it. It's pretty far south of Gail, Texas. It's about 500 miles away from my house, about an eight-hour drive. How am I going to get all the way down there without my mom getting suspicious? Then I remember Andrew will insist on going too. It is Friday, so I could tell my mom that we're going on a weekend trip to the beach. Next, I look up hotels. Before I book the rooms, I call Andrew.

"Hello?" Andrew asks, answering my call.

"Hey, I found him," I reply.

"Ever? Where?" Andrew asks.

"He's at the NAS Corpus Christi Naval Base," I reply.

As soon as I said that, I hear shuffling and then typing in the background.

"Oh man, that's like eight hours away from here," Andrew

says.

"I found a decent priced hotel, and I'm about to book two rooms. You interested in having a beach weekend?" I ask trying not to giggle.

"Let's do it! I need to get out," Andrew says with a laugh.

"Alright, I just booked us our rooms."

"Cool. I guess we're leaving today?" Andrew asks.

"Yeah, that would be best," I reply.

"Okay, I'll pick you up in about an hour," Andrew advises.

"Perfect, see you then," I respond, then I hang up.

I quickly run downstairs and grab a small bag to pack in. Then I notice my mom grabbing her keys and walking towards the door.

"Hey, Mom!" I shout to her.

"Yeah?" my mom asks.

"Andrew and I are going on a beach, weekend trip a few hours south of here. We'll be back probably sometime Sunday. That's okay, right?" I ask hoping she'll say yes.

"Wait, this is an overnight trip?" my mom asks with a concerned look.

"Yes, and I have two rooms booked," I inform.

"Okay, but I'm not sure if I'm comfortable with you and him together so far away and alone," my mom says hesitantly.

"Mom, we're not going to be alone. We'll be visiting the beach, shops, and tourist centers. I'll be sure to tell you when we get there and update you. Please," I plead.

She's staring at me with her arms crossed and deep in thought. Then she sighs and smiles.

"Fine, but you better let me know when you get there and send some pictures of you guys at the beach," my mom says warmly.

"Thank you for trusting me, Mom," I sigh in relief and hug her goodbye.

"Of course. Just be mindful and careful," my mom responds.

"I will," I assure.

When my mom leaves the house and drives off, I head upstairs to quickly pack a bag. I realize I won't need much for an overnight trip, but I decide to pack a swimsuit in case we do actually go to the beach. I've never been a good packer. I usually just throw a variety of clothes in my bag and hope for the best. This trip is much different though. It's no vacation; it's a mission. I stuff a hairbrush and other hair products in my bag and zip it up. Since we'll be by the beach, these products keep my wavy hair tame and soft. After I finish, I bring my bag downstairs into the kitchen to wait for Andrew. Then I find a cooler bag in a closet and begin packing snacks and drinks for the long drive. As soon as I finish, I hear squeaking brakes outside. I head towards the door, anticipating Andrew's arrival. I open the door, once I hear knocking.

"Hey," I greet, seeing Andrew standing on the deck.

"Hey, you ready to go?" Andrew asks.

"Yeah, let me just grab my bags," I respond.

I run into the kitchen and grab my small bag and the cooler. Then, I run to Andrew's car. I load my small bag in the trunk but keep the cooler bag with me in the front. Andrew pulls out of the driveway, and we're off!

An hour and a half passes, as we talk about school and future career ideas.

"Not to completely change the subject, but how did you find out where Ever is?" Andrew asks.

"Ever made another vision for me last night and told me where he is. Although, he isn't exactly in the naval base," I answer.

"Umm, what?" Andrew asks.

"Ever said the base made a custom cell for him," I reply in a nervous tone.

"Okay, where?" Andrew asks.

"In the water," I answer, while I begin to giggle.

"The water?" Andrew shouts.

"Yes," I respond laughing out loud at Andrew's expression.

"How are we going to get in there?" Andrew asks looking at me with a confused look.

"Great question. I'm still trying to figure that out," I say catching my breath from laughing.

"You haven't thought of it till now?" Andrew asks in a nervous chuckle.

"I figured we could use the car ride to figure it out," I explain with a smile.

"Oh great," Andrew grunts, as he shakes his head with a smile.

We're silent for a while.

"I wonder if they have tours at this base," I state thinking out loud.

"That could work," Andrew replies.

I begin looking up on my phone if the base has tours, and they do. Although, they are all booked today, but fortunately, I find an opening tomorrow.

"Hey, there's a tour tomorrow at 1:00 pm," I inform him.

"Great! Let's do that," Andrew responds.

Another few hours pass, and Andrew pulls off the highway to an exit where he can get gas. As he refuels, I go inside the gas station to use the restroom. After I wash my hands, I begin fixing my messy, brown hair in the mirror, thankful that I brought along my hairbrush and hair products. Suddenly the bathroom stall doors begin to rattle, then the entire bathroom begins to shake. The ceiling above me begins to crack, and dust starts to sprinkle everywhere. I hear people screaming outside. The thundering from the shaking is so loud that I can't even think to move. All that I can move are my eyes, and they're darting in every direction. Then my eyes catch on something. My arm is glowing again. The burning needles return, but this time, they're more intense. I shriek in pain and collapse to the floor. I squeeze myself into a ball and continue to scream in pain. Pieces of ceiling begin falling all around me. Then, one piece falls onto my ankle and I scream even louder. I hear a faint voice cutting through the thundering gas station.

"Raya!" I hear.

Suddenly Andrew throws the bathroom door open and finds me on the ground shrieking in misery. He rushes over to me and quickly picks me up then runs out of the gas station with me in his arms. I hide my glowing arm under my other arm as he continues to run, but he sees it when we reach his car in the shaking parking lot.

"What do you want me to do?" Andrew shouts, referring to my glowing arm.

"Don't touch it!" I yell back, remembering Ever's warning.

Everything continues to shake with no sign of stopping. I see panicked people running in the street. Light posts fall over, and cars swerve in an attempt to dodge them. The shaking needs to stop.

"Ever," I whisper to myself. "Ever."

The shaking slows, then finally, it stops. My ears ring a little from the thundering, but eventually that stops too.

"Are you okay?" I ask Andrew.

"I'm fine, but you're not!" Andrew announces while pointing to my swollen, blue ankle.

"Oh, ouch. Well at least my arm's not glowing," I say with a small grin.

"Raya," Andrew sighs.

Andrew places me in the passenger seat of his car, then he runs back into the gas station. After a few minutes, he comes out with an icepack and hands it to me.

"Did you buy this?" I ask.

"No, I said I was going to sue them for neglecting their old building unless they'd give me this icepack for free. They agreed, so I took it," Andrew explains as we drive off.

"Are you serious?" I ask laughing.

"Yeah," Andrew replies with a chuckle.

After many more hours in the car, we finally pull into the hotel at around 9:00 pm. Andrew unloads the trunk, while I try standing up on my swollen ankle.

"Raya, please stop," Andrew advises, after he pulls the last bag out of the trunk.

"I'm fine. It looks worse than it is," I inform, as I limp a little towards my bag.

"I'm carrying this," Andrew states as he takes the bag out of my reach.

"Fine," I say with a laugh.

I check in at the front desk of the hotel, and the clerk hands us our room keys. Then Andrew and I go up the elevator and find our rooms, which are right across from each other. I unlock my door and hold it open for Andrew, while he places my bag next to my bed.

"Well, if you need anything just knock," Andrew says, as he walks into his room and closes the door.

I walk into my room, then close and lock my door. I get ready for bed and then ice my ankle while I watch TV. After a moment, I text my mom letting her know that we made it safely. A few minutes later, I turn off the TV and throw the icepack into the small hotel freezer. I lay back in bed and close my heavy eyes. My body begins to relax, and I finally fall asleep.

chapter five

THE BREAK IN

My sleepy eyes finally begin to open. When I stand up on the old hotel carpet my ankle begins to throb some, but it's manageable. I'm not sure how the day's going to go. How are Andrew and I going to find Ever? It's a navy base, so there will be personnel everywhere. Maybe Ever can help us.

When I finish getting ready, I hear a knock on the door.

"Hey, you ready to get some breakfast in the lobby?" Andrew asks, as soon as I open my door.

"Yeah, let's go," I reply.

Andrew and I head straight to the breakfast buffet and fill our plates with as much food as we can. We find a table near a window and sit down.

"Have you figured out a plan?" Andrew asks.

"To get Ever? No," I respond.

"Well, we better come up with a plan fast," Andrew says with his mouth full of bacon.

"Yeah—I'm hoping we will see a 'restricted area' sign while we are on the tour," I explain.

"That's a good point. Do you think you can communicate with Ever? If that's a thing," Andrew says with a grin.

"I can try. We'll see," I say with a laugh.

"Let's get to the base early and look around," Andrew suggests.

"Yes, let's do that!" I answer.

When we finish our breakfast, we discuss different ideas and strategies that could help us find Ever. After a while of talking and killing time, we head back up to our rooms to grab a few things, then we rush down to Andrew's car. The base is only a few miles away, so we get there an hour before the tour starts.

Once we park, we get out of the car and walk down to the beach. The sand is cool to the touch, and the ocean breeze throws my hair around. I begin scanning my eyes across the water to find any sign of manmade buildings under the surface. I can't see anything in the water that looks like the cell Ever described; there is just endless blue water.

"Ever, where are you?" I whisper to myself.

After a few more minutes of scanning the horizon,

Andrew and I walk over to the base entrance. When we reach the entrance, there are two armed soldiers guarding the doors. They asked for our IDs, and when we show them, they let us through.

"That's weird, armed soldiers at the door?" Andrew comments in an annoyed tone.

Once we walk inside, I begin investigating my surroundings. I see a few other visitors, some desks, and cracks in the walls, but nothing that hints where Ever may be. One of the visitors tries going through a door, but a soldier instructs him to wait for the tour. This place is so restricted. How are we going to find Ever in here?

"Hey, Raya, look at this," Andrew says, while pointing to a map of the base plastered on the wall.

Andrew and I investigate the map, but the longer I look, the more discouraged I become.

"There's nothing in the water or even near the water," I state in a disappointed tone.

"Maybe that's what they want us to think," Andrew adds.

I begin to feel like this was a stupid idea. What was I thinking?

"Ever, I'm here. I don't know where to go or where to start looking for you," I say to myself.

I unexpectedly feel my arm start to tingle. I glance down at it, and I can see a slight, white glow coming from under my skin. Then my eyes become cold like ice. Suddenly I hear a voice telling me to look around, so I walk around the only room I have access to and try to look at everything. Then a soldier announces that everyone in the 1:00 tour needs to line up, as the tour is about to start. As we follow the small crowd of visitors, I stand directly behind Andrew. My eyes are still cold, so I continue to scan everything around me.

"Do you think Ever knows we're here?" Andrew whispers to me.

"Yes, I think he sees we're here too," I reply.

"Sees?" Andrew asks, looking very confused.

"I think he's looking through my eyes," I clarify.

"Okay. Don't say that out loud, because you sound crazy," Andrew advises trying not to laugh.

"Yeah, thanks," I respond giggling.

During the tour, I glance over my shoulder, and I see a 'restricted area' sign. The sign is bolted to a door with a keypad and guards blocking it. The voice in my head suddenly speaks saying, "That's it." I nudge Andrew and gesture towards the door.

"That *is* it, isn't it?" Andrew asks, when he looks at the door.

"Yes, we need to get in there," I reply nervously.

Andrew asks the tour guide about the door, but the tour guide just says it's classified and continues with the tour. I sigh in disappointment as I glance down at my arm again, and it stops glowing. Then my eyes return to normal.

"Wait," I say out loud.

"What?" Andrew asks, stopping suddenly and looking at me.

Suddenly, terrible shaking begins. The roaring thunder comes back, and the cracks on the walls open up more. My arm sears in pain like burning knives and needles again. I clench my arm and begin to yell in agony while Andrew hunches over me trying to protect me from falling rubble.

"We have to go for it!" Andrew announces to me.

When we begin running towards the trembling door, the soldiers raise their guns at us. Andrew puts his arm in front of me to stop me, but the thunderous shaking causes the ceiling to collapse and forces the door open. The soldiers jump out of the way of most of the debris, but they're still covered in rubble. Andrew runs through the doorway while I follow behind him. Unexpectedly, a hand grabs my left arm, and I am yanked to a stop. Then I realize a soldier grabbed my glowing arm. I gasp and yell, "No!" I watch in horror as every vein in the soldier's body glows in pure white. The soldier screams in pain, but he can't let go. Then I begin to feel the soldier's pulse slowing down inside of me, like it's my own, and I can sense how terrified he is.

"Let go!" I scream at the soldier, with tears running down

my face.

Andrew grabs my right arm, and tries to pull me away, but I won't budge. I scream to the soldier once more, but when I see his eyes become still and shining white, I fear it is too late to help him. Suddenly, the thundering sound and shaking ceases, and where I saw the vibration of the walls of the base, I now see transparent people, like Ever. The roaring and shaking has turned into voices. I remember the mysterious statement Ever made the first day I met him, "I can hear them again! I can see them again!" Those voice were calling Ever's name that day, just like the transparent people are doing now. The voices are so overwhelming; I can't bare it.

"They won't stop!" I scream.

"Raya!" Andrew yells.

I frantically try to pull away from the suffering soldier again, but I cannot move. The soldier continues to scream in agony, until the glowing white comes beaming out of his eyes and veins. Then a sudden white flash shatters the soldier into nothing. The voices and the transparent people disappear, and the thundering, shaking sounds return. I look back at Andrew, and he's in shock.

"I think I just killed that soldier!" I scream horrified.

"Just keep running!" Andrew shouts back, trying to forget what he just witnessed.

Andrew and I continue to run down the dark, shaking

hall. I try to focus on running, but all I can feel is my searing arm and the feeling of the soldier's last heartbeat, until he lit up into nothing. Tears cloud my vision, so I stop. Andrew notices and comes back to me. The roaring thunder continues, while Andrew yells something to me. He grabs my right arm and pulls me to continue running, so I do. Then I hear yelling guards behind us.

"Faster!" Andrew announces.

"We have to lose them!" I implore.

We keep running. I think we must have traveled three miles by now through these endless hallways.

Abruptly, I hear a voice in my head saying "disappear," and I suddenly feel light as a feather. Andrew turns his head towards me and stops without warning; I nearly run into him.

"Raya?" Andrew yells over the shaking.

"What?" I shout back.

Andrew continues to look around.

"Where are you, Raya?" Andrew yells in a panic.

"I'm right here!" I shriek back.

I jump right in front of him, and no response. I hear the soldiers approaching. Then I recall the word spoken in my head, "disappear." Am I invisible? I grab Andrew's hand, and he finally locks eyes with me.

"Raya?" Andrew shouts with a confused look.

I pull him against the thundering wall in the dark

hallway. Andrew and I lean flat against the wall, as the charging soldiers run past. I no longer feel light, so I let go of Andrew's hand.

"What is going on?" Andrew exclaims in a terrified voice.

"Just keep running!" I yell in return.

We continue running down the dark, thundering hall. Out of nowhere we come up on another hallway going left. The voice comes back again and instructs me to turn left; I halt to a stop.

"Andrew, stop! We need to go this way!" I announce over the deafening rumbles.

"How do you know?" Andrew shouts.

"Follow me!" I yell running down the hallway.

I feel out of breath, but my adrenaline keeps me going. Where could Ever be? We've been running for what seems like hours. The thunderous shaking doesn't stop. The constant trembling and rattling of the base are making me stumble over my own feet. Suddenly, red lights begin flashing and a roaring alarm begins to go off all around us. An intercom echoes the announcement, "Tsunami alert!" repeatedly.

"Tsunami alert?" I shriek in disbelief.

I keep on running, trying to ignore the roaring alarm, then Andrew stops unexpectedly in front of a huge door broken at the hinges. I thought to say something, but Andrew continues running, so I follow. We make it to another door.

The walls thunder louder, and water drips all around us. Then I hear yelling from inside the room. It must be Ever.

"Ever!" I scream at the door.

Andrew starts banging on the door. Abruptly, the door begins to warp and move, so Andrew and I jump to the side. The door breaks, and I rush inside, leaving Andrew behind; I see Ever.

"Ever, we have to get out of here!" I shout to him.

Before Ever can answer, I glance out the window and see a massive swirl under the surface of the water coming directly toward us. The tsunami! Ever sees me look that way and grabs my glowing hand. He begins running towards the door to leave. As he pulls me, I peer behind me, and I see the room on the verge of being crushed by the wave. I become terrified, so I freeze like a statue. Ever's forced to stop. He turns around and picks me up and starts running again.

"Where's Andrew?" I yell up to Ever.

"He is behind me!" Ever replies.

"Raya, I'm okay! We're almost out!" Andrew shouts to me.

The water dripping from the ceiling has increased to a pouring rain, and the shaking still has not stopped. Why hasn't Ever stopped it? I look up to Ever to say something, but his eyes are blazing in glowing white, so I stay quiet.

We finally make it to the room where we started the

base tour. Ever puts me down, and I see the huge wave approaching. I tremble in fear, and my head begins to feel light. I start to fall, but Ever catches me. Andrew tries to help, but Ever sets me under a desk, to try and shield me from the oncoming wave. Water starts rushing in through the windows; the tsunami's here. Under the desk, Ever presses me up against the wall. I begin to sob in terror, and I press my face against his chest. Ever wraps his arms around me, as I feel the water rise.

"Wait, where's Andrew?" I scream.

Ever begins to look over his shoulder. Then I see Andrew running towards another desk as the tsunami crashes through the wall.

"Andrew!" I shout to him.

"Raya!" Andrew yells from the faint distance.

Andrew is swept away by the force of the wave. Water is now over my head. I look to Ever, and he has a serious look on his face, with his eyes continuing to glow with white. I'm losing my breath. I glance to Ever, and he notices me suffering. He clenches my searing, glowing hand, and the white signs begin to blink. Miraculously, I can breathe normally. The water around us starts to swirl and whip me back and forth, so Ever holds me down more firmly to keep me still. The pressure over us keeps getting heavier and heavier, and the chill of the water is making me shiver. I look to Ever, and he locks eyes with me. My insides begin to rumble, and my eyes suddenly roll back into the back of my head. Now it's all black.

chapter six
ANDREW

My eyes slowly peel open. I look around and see a cloudless sky. I feel a brisk sea breeze, and my soggy clothes are sticking to my wet skin. Then I hear sirens ringing in what seems like every direction. Finally, I try to sit up.

"Hey, be careful. You may have been injured, so try not to move too much," Ever advises, helping me sit up.

There's no shaking, and my arm isn't glowing. Although, there is debris everywhere I look. Then I remember Andrew, and my chest suddenly feels like lead.

"Where's Andrew?" I shout, about to cry.

"His bod—he has not been found yet," Ever replies hesitantly.

"What?" I scream. "Andrew! Andrew!" I scream again, with tears running down my face.

"Shhh. You are okay," Ever says trying to calm me down.

Ever cups my face in his hands and wipes my tears away. A few minutes pass, and EMTs come over to check and see if I'm okay. While they're examining me, I glance over to Ever, who has backed away. He doesn't seem comfortable with the EMTs near me. Every time an EMT touches me, he tenses up. The EMTs finally finish and run over to other victims of the tsunami. Then I hear an exhale.

"Umm, you okay?" I ask Ever.

"Sure," Ever replies in a puff.

"Ever?" I ask.

"I just do not like people messing with you," Ever responds squeezing his fists.

"Ever, they were trying to make sure I am alright," I inform a bit puzzled.

"You do not know that," Ever says, as his eyes flicker from white, then back to his normal dark blue.

I roll my eyes with annoyance, but then I see a police officer. I look to Ever, and he notices my desire to go to the officer. Ever comes close to me again.

"Ever, no," I state firmly. "You may be a powerful being, but unlike you, I know this Earth and how it works."

Ever doesn't say anything but nods showing that he understands. Then I run over to the officer, while Ever's close behind me.

"Officer!" I yell.

"Yes, can I help?" the officer asks.

"Yeah, have you seen my friend, Andrew?" I ask.

"I'm sorry, ma'am, but there's still a lot of rubble to go through and many bodies to identify. I'll keep a look out for an Andrew, though. We've identified a few victims and made some rescues, so hopefully we'll find your friend," the officer replies.

"Okay, thank you," I respond as my lip begins to quiver.

Ever comes up behind me and places his hand on my shoulder.

"We will find him," Ever says in a deep, warm tone.

I begin shivering uncontrollably. My lips turn blue, and my finger tips are almost numb.

"I want to search for Andrew," I state looking at Ever.

"That is fine, but you need warmer attire," Ever informs with a concerned expression.

Andrew's car was washed away from the wave, so Ever and I walk to the hotel. It's not but a few miles from where we were. The hotel is pretty damaged, but nothing compared to the navy base. Once we make it inside, Ever follows me to my room. Before I could ask him to wait, Ever saw me open my door and immediately moved to the side to stand guard outside my door.

"Just give me a few minutes," I say.

"Take your time," Ever responds.

I walk into my hotel room and close the door. Then I change from my soggy, cold clothes to warm, dry ones. A few minutes later, I walk out to meet Ever outside my door.

"I'm ready," I say to him.

"Good, but I ask one thing," Ever informs.

"What?" I ask.

"Please, do not wander off by yourself. I cannot bare to see you get hurt again," Ever advises with a fierce expression.

"I won't," I reply.

Ever appears satisfied with my response, so I begin walking to the lobby, while he follows. Once we exit the hotel, we start for the navy base. Ever and I are almost to the destroyed base, as I trudge along, wallowing in my thoughts. I never should have asked Andrew to come with me. If I hadn't invited him, he wouldn't have been swept away or–killed. This is all my fault; I'm a terrible friend. Suddenly my arm begins to tingle.

"Raya, you should not think like that," Ever says.

I stare at him in shock.

"You may think that you are the reason for his disappearance, but in reality, he would have just followed you here. From what I have seen, Andrew would be there for you no matter what," Ever explains.

"You're probably right," I reply with tears running down my cheeks.

Ever looks at me and grins.

"I'm guessing the reason why my arm was tingling was because you were reading my thoughts," I mention, trying to laugh away my tears.

"Ha, well, yes," Ever responds with a chuckle.

That's the first time I've heard Ever laugh. The deep, warm sound of his laugh makes me cheer up a little.

We finally make it to the base. There are many EMTs and officers looking through the rubble, but I haven't seen one military personnel anywhere. My only guess is that none of them survived. Ever and I begin to search everywhere in the surrounding area for any sign of Andrew. So far, there's no sign of him.

Two hours pass by, and still no sign of Andrew. I plop to the ground and cry into my hands, so Ever paces to my side.

"I just hope Andrew's alive, Ever," I say balling with tears.

"Raya, be hopeful and keep searching. We still have lots of ground to cover," Ever informs while putting his arm behind my back, trying to comfort me.

Eventually, I get up to continue looking. I check behind every large rock, tree, and bush but still nothing. Suddenly, I feel a small part of me feeling depressed, but it's not me. I look at my arm, and it's glowing again. Then the burning needles return. I clench it trying to carry on the search, but where's Ever? I turn around, and he's leaning up against a tree, so I run over to him.

"Ever, what's wrong?" I ask in concern.

Ever lifts his dark, blue eyes up to mine, and they're shiny with tears. Then he slowly hands me a piece of cloth. I take it from his hand and investigate it.

"This is Andrew's shirt!" I shout with a gasp.

Ever nods.

"Raya, I do not know why you were blaming yourself about Andrew. You really should be blaming me. After all, I should have just stood there like a statue, like I did with the other guests at the museum. Then this never would have happened," Ever says with his head down.

"Maybe, but it doesn't matter," I say. "Aghh!" I shriek as the pain in my arm spikes.

Ever notices I'm in pain and sees my glowing arm. He leans off the tree and places both hands on either side of my left arm. I feel a sudden cooling sensation, then the glowing, alien, signs sink away.

"Better?" Ever asks.

"Yes, thank you," I sigh in relief. "Andrew has to be here somewhere if you found part of his shirt," I say in enthusiasm.

Then I start searching again but with more urgency. I finally have hope that Andrew's close. He has to be here. A few minutes later, I find an open area. I look behind a rock, and there he is!

"Ever, I found him! Andrew!" I shout.

I jump to Andrew's side. He's lying on his back, and he has bruises on his arms, legs, and face. I check for a pulse on his neck, and I feel some movement.

"He's alive!" I announce.

Ever is suddenly by my side. I place my hand on Andrew's cheek; it's ice cold and wet. His clothes are all torn up and mangled. Then I look at his chest, and it's barely rising and falling.

"Ever, we have to get help!" I say in a panic.

Ever immediately lifts Andrew in his arms. Then he runs back to the navy base, and I follow. As we run, I see Andrew's feet bounce and dangle lifelessly as Ever carries him. My vision begins to cloud with tears, then I see the flashing lights of the emergency vehicles.

"Help!" I yell at the top of my lungs.

EMTs start sprinting towards us with a stretcher. When we reach them, Ever gently lays Andrew's lifeless body onto the bed. The EMTs load Andrew into the ambulance, and I jump in.

"Ever, come on!" I say in a panic.

Ever jumps in, and the ambulance rushes to the hospital. The EMTs are hovering over Andrew with needles and other objects trying to keep him alive and breathing. My chest feels heavy as I watch, and I start breathing heavily. Ever grabs my hand and squeezes it. I look into his rich, dark, blue eyes as he looks into mine. My insides don't start to rumble like before, but they feel soft and relaxed. I smile in relief, and Ever smiles back. I lean up against his shoulder but keep a close eye on Andrew.

Eventually the ambulance pulls into the hospital, and Andrew is rushed inside. Ever and I follow behind him, but Andrew is brought into an area that we are not allowed in. Ever and I shuffle into the waiting room to sit and wait. Minutes pass, I feel restless, hoping that Andrew is okay. I glance out the window, seeing it's getting dark, and let out an unexpected yawn.

"Raya, you can lay down on this bench," Ever suggests.

"I can't sleep," I respond mid-yawn.

"You can at least rest. It has been a long day," Ever adds.

"I guess that would be nice," I say.

Ever scoots down the bench, while I lift my feet and lay down. I feel my body relax, so I close my eyes. Hours pass by, and I am awoken by a hand rubbing my arm.

"Hmm," I mutter half asleep.

"The doctor is here," Ever says softly.

"The doctor!" I repeat, immediately sitting up.

The doctor smiles at me, as I try to keep my tired eyes open.

"Sorry for the long wait. It's a miracle that he's alive.

Andrew had a lot of water in his lungs and has multiple minor hairline fractures in his ribs, legs, and arms. He was also without oxygen for a long period of time, and his brain has swollen as a result of a sudden blow. Andrew is in a coma for now. I don't know when he'll wake up, but he's stable," the doctor explains.

I have no words; I'm frozen and terrified. What if he never wakes up?

"Can we see him?" Ever asks.

"Yes, follow me," the doctor responds before he walks away.

Ever grabs my hand and leads my statue-like body to follow the doctor. We walk down hallway after hallway. The cool air in the halls makes me shiver, but finally, we arrive at Andrew's room. Ever and I walk in and see Andrew lying on the bed. He's connected to what seems like every machine possible. I step over to his side and place my hand on his cheek. It's cold and stiff.

"I'm so sorry," I whisper.

I have tears in my eyes as I look at Ever, who's found a comfortable chair.

"Raya, they have a bed in here. You should sleep," Ever suggests.

"You're right," I reply while wiping the tears away.

I stumble over to the bed and lie down. I twist myself in

the covers and blankets, and I close my eyes. My mind drifts, then I fall into a deep sleep.

chapter seven

EVER

Sunrays glimmer through the window into my sleepy eyes. I sit up and try to rub the sleep out of my face. I glance to Ever, who's still fast asleep in the comfy chair. I guess beings like him sleep too. Something's different about him, but I can't figure it out. Then I look at Andrew; I walk over to the side of his bed. I stare at his pale, still face. I peer to the machines keeping him alive and breathing. The beeping, pumping, and groaning of the machines cause shivers to climb up my spine. I place my hand on Andrew's and squeeze it tight.

"Andrew, I don't know if you can hear me, but I'm sorry. This is all my fault. —I just need you to do one more thing for me. I need you to hold on and wake up. I need you, Andrew, please wake up," I whisper to him, as I clench his hand.

Tears begin running down my face. I catch them with my

fingers, then I run out of the room. I quickly walk down the hospital hallway and find a bathroom. I run in and lock the door. I stand in front of the mirror and watch the tears scatter down my cheeks. I turn on the cold water from the faucet and cup the water in my shaking hands; I splash the refreshing water on my face. I feel a quick relief run through my body, but the worry and sadness soon returns. Suddenly my arm begins blinking, but I'm not in pain. Then I hear knocking on the door.

"Raya?" Ever asks from outside the door.

"Ever, please go away," I plead while grabbing paper towels and wiping my face.

I look up in the mirror again, and I see the door open with Ever standing in the doorway. Once I see him, I turn around with my eyes pink, and tears running down my cheeks again. Then Ever comes over to me and wipes the tears away.

"Raya, I know you do not like to cry in front of anyone, but you have every right to," Ever says in a warm tone.

I let go, and the tears pour down my face. I wrap my arms around Ever's neck, and he wraps his arms around my waist while I cry into his shoulder. My arm continues to blink, but I still feel no pain. Ever holds me tighter, and I finally begin to calm down. I felt like I was holding back a tsunami inside of me, and I finally released it. I let out a sigh of relief. Then my left arm stops blinking and returns to normal.

"Thank you," I whisper into Ever's shoulder.

"Just relax," Ever says in a soothing tone.

Ever starts to release his hold on me, and I do the same. When we eventually let go, I turn around and grab another paper towel and wipe my tears away again. Then I begin to smile and blush at Ever; because I feel a little embarrassed. Ever notices and chuckles a little with a smile.

"Are you ready to go back to Andrew's room?" Ever asks.

"Yeah," I reply with a small frog in my throat.

I exit the bathroom with Ever close behind. When we make it back to Andrew's room, I sit down in a chair next to him, and Ever sits back in his comfy chair. I sigh in relief again and lean back in my seat.

An hour passes, and Andrew hasn't changed. Ever and I have been sitting quietly and waiting. I look out the hospital room door, and I see doctors and nurses walking by. Then I see a mom and a little girl pass by.

"It's Sunday! My mom thinks Andrew and I are coming home!" I announce in a panic.

Ever just about jumps out of his skin when I shout.

"Raya, do not yell like that. We are in a hospital," Ever exclaims, startled.

"What am I going to tell her? That Andrew's basically dead in the hospital, and I was underwater in a tsunami! Or that I'm with a 546-year-old alien!" I yell.

"Raya, quiet. I am not an alien, and why are you shouting my age in a public building? My years are interpreted in a different way, so I am really 19 in your world. Do not alarm people," Ever says in annoyance.

"I'm sorry, I just don't know what I'm going to tell her," I respond anxiously.

"Tell her that you had to extend the trip, because of the tsunami traffic. I mean I am sure it is all over the news," Ever suggests.

"That's perfect!" I shout.

"Raya!" Ever says quickly.

"Sorry," I reply.

I pull out my phone and begin dialing my mom's number while I walk out of the room. It's ringing, then she answers.

"Raya! I've been so worried! Are you guys okay? I saw the tsunami on the news!" my mom says in a worried tone.

"Everything's okay, Mom, don't worry," I reassure hoping she wouldn't catch my bluff. "Andrew and I have to extend the trip because of all the tsunami obstacles, so we should be back, umm, sometime this week," I continue.

"Alright. Please, stay safe! What have you guys been doing?" my mom asks.

"We're fine! We went to the beach, and we've been going to other places too. We were really enjoying the trip, until all of this craziness happened," I reply.

"Oh good! Well, be safe and come back when you can. Hopefully I'll see you when you get home," my mom adds.

"We will! Wait, why?" I ask.

"I'm going out of town Wednesday for a conference, and I'll be gone for two weeks," my mom responds.

"Oh," I mutter, thinking I'll be home without my mom, so she won't be suspicious of anything.

"Yeah, so I guess I'll see you in a few weeks. Anyways, be careful! Love you," my mom says.

"I will and love you too!" I respond, then I hang up the phone.

I walk back into the room and sit back into the chair. Then I see out of the corner of my eye that my arm suddenly stops glowing. I look over to Ever with a smug look.

"I'm guessing the reason my arm was glowing was because you were listening and reading my mind," I suggest.

"Correct," Ever replies laughing.

We sit quietly for a little bit. Then I begin thinking of what happened at the base with the soldiers and the tsunami. I want an explanation from Ever.

"When I was in the base, a soldier grabbed my glowing arm. I experienced everything he felt and saw. I felt his last heartbeat. I also saw transparent people like you; they were calling your name," I explain. "Wait, why don't you look transparent?" I ask realizing why he seemed different.

"First, let me explain my transparency. I am not transparent right now, because I am borrowing your human state, so my appearance looks normal to you," Ever replies.

"You're borrowing my human state, which must be less powerful than your own. That's why my arm doesn't hurt when it glows, right?" I ask.

"Exactly. My being form and your human form are somewhat the same, but my form has the glow, which provides me with an extra dose of power. Because of that, you, as a human with weak senses, see me as transparent and can be harmed. Now about the other transparent people like me. Do you remember that I said I am not from your Earth?" Ever asks.

"Yeah," I answer.

"I live here, but when I am home in my dimension, you observe me, here, as the vibrational sounds you hear and the vibrations you see. It is difficult to detect us with frail human senses, but when beings, like me, cause vibrations from our glows, it creates movement that can be felt here. When you touched that soldier, you absorbed his human strength through the glow of your arm, which gave you more power than a human already possesses to see a glimpse into, as you humans would say, another dimension," Ever explains.

"Another dimension?" I ask in disbelief.

"Yes. Those beings you saw are looking for me. Humans

have the military, but my kind has the Dimensionary. We travel to different dimensions and research the beings who live there. I was assigned to Earth. Although, there were some complications. I was supposed to be able to communicate with my team at home, but I cannot. That is why they are calling for me. Our technology must have identified my distant vibrations and located me. My team most likely responded to that location and sent off trembles to get my attention. They came too close to me which created friction between the dimensions and that caused me pain, making vibrations. Our trembles combined caused the tsunami," Ever explains.

"Oh wow. When are you supposed to go back?" I ask, trying to wrap my head around everything.

"That is the thing. I do not know if I can. I am still trying to figure that out," Ever informs.

"Hmm. Do you want to go back?" I ask.

Ever looks up at me and grins.

"Well, not really; since I met you," Ever replies smiling at me.

I begin blushing and smile.

"You make a good point," I add laughing. "Don't you want to see your friends and family again?" I continue.

"Yes, I do. That is why I am trying to figure out if it is even possible to go back," Ever says no longer smiling.

"Is your family similar to the families here?" I ask.

"Yeah, I have a mother, a father, and a younger brother," Ever replies.

"Really? What are their names?" I ask in curiosity.

"My mother's name is Izel, my father is Willem, and my brother is Evin. Our last name is Winters," Ever explains with a smile.

"Wow. Can I ask how old they are?"

"It is going to sound crazy to you," Ever says laughing.

"What is it?" I laugh.

"My mother is 1,090, my father is 1,092, and my brother is 518," Ever replies.

"That's crazy," I say in shock.

"Like I said," Ever says with a chuckle. "What about your family?" Ever asks.

"Mine? Well, it's only me and my mom. My mom's name is Alivia. My dad died when I was nine; his name was Logan. Oh, and our last name is Fawn," I explain.

"I am so sorry, Raya. Can I ask how he died?" Ever asks hesitantly.

"Yeah, it was a long time ago. He died of cancer. It was a long battle, and sadly he lost," I reply.

"I am sorry. That must have been hard for you," Ever says.

"Yes, it was," I respond nodding. "Well, I finally know something about the mysterious Ever," I say with a soft giggle in an attempt to change the subject.

"Ha, yes you do," Ever replies with a laugh.

We're smiling at each other until a nurse comes in.

"There you are. I came in earlier to take some tests, but you guys weren't here," the nurse explains.

"Oh, sorry. What were the tests?" I ask with hope.

"They were tests to see if there's any progress with Andrew's brain. The tests on his brain are showing good improvement, which indicates that the swelling is decreasing, however, it will take some time for it to fully recover. I am hopeful he will wake up soon," the nurse explains smiling.

"Really?" I ask happily.

"Yes. Let me know if you guys need anything," the nurse advises before she walks out.

"Thank you," Ever responds.

"So, he's going to be okay," I say in excitement.

"I guess so," Ever replies with a grin.

chapter eight

WAKE UP

It has been two days of anxious waiting. I stare at Andrew hoping for him to wake up. I sit up from my make-shift bed, and look over to Ever to ask him something, but he's not there.

"Hmm," I mutter to myself, that's weird.

I lay back down again, and suddenly, I hear a bizarre noise. It's a thump, and then dragging noise, repeatedly. It's getting closer. Now, I hear trickling. Water maybe? My eyes are open wide, fear swirling in my stomach, and my fingers are numb in distress. I slowly sit up, and my lip is shivering. I dart my eyes toward the strange noise. My jaw drops. It's the soldier that I killed at the naval base. He drags his foot as he moves closer. There's blood dripping from his mouth, neck, and ears and onto the floor. His clothes are smeared with blood. The soldier locks his eyes on mine. His eyes are black. I quickly scoot back up against the wall on the bed, shaking.

"What do you want?" I blurt out terrified.

No response. The soldier continues walking closer, but then stops and looks over at Andrew's still body.

"No, stop," I try to say firmly, but I'm still shaking.

The soldier stands over Andrew. I start to move off my bed, but the soldier snaps his head towards me, so I freeze. As he glares at me, blood drips from his mouth onto Andrew. Then the soldier looks back to Andrew and places his hand on Andrew's neck.

"No!" I shout in a panic.

The soldier continues to grip Andrew's neck. I suddenly hear a loud cracking and then an oozing sound. Then the soldier takes his hand off of Andrew, and there's blood dripping off the soldier's hand.

"No, Andrew!" I scream with tears spilling down my cheeks.

The soldier walks in front of me, blood dripping to the floor.

"Why?" I ask sobbing.

"You did this to me, now you can see and feel the pain you put me through," the soldier informs, while grabbing my neck with his bloody hand.

Andrew's hot blood drips down my neck. The soldier tightens his grip on me, and I gasp for air. I feel immense pressure on the veins, tendons, and muscles in my neck.

"Please," I barely get out.

"You never gave me a chance," the soldier replies, as blood is *spat onto my face.*

There's a loud snap, then darkness.

"Ah," I yelp while sitting up in my bed, gasping for air. Ever suddenly flashes to my side.

"Raya, what is wrong?" Ever asks in a panic. Ever squats down in front of me, as I frantically look around the room. No blood and no soldier. Then I look at Andrew, he's still breathing and alive. I grab my neck; no damage has been done. Finally, I glance to Ever. His warm eyes are looking into my teary ones. Then my arm starts tingling. In a flash, I see my entire dream cross over Ever's dark blue eyes. His face is as still as stone.

"Nightmare, huh?" Ever asks with a dreary expression.

I nod. Then I take a deep breath and exhale, trying to calm myself down. Suddenly, my arm starts glowing brighter and Ever takes my glowing hand.

"Need some help?" Ever asks in a warm voice, trying to help calm me down.

I nod again with a tear running down my cheek. Ever's blue eyes turn beaming white, and his hand, that is holding mine, has white, glowing, alien signs rising from his skin and traveling up his entire arm. I feel relief rushing through my body like a wave. My quivering lip relaxes, and the fear inside me melts away. The tears that were once lodged in my eyes disappear. I feel content. Gradually, Ever's arm stops glowing, and his eyes return back to their rich, dark blue, and my arm stops glowing. Ever releases my hand and sits next to me. I sigh in relief and smile.

"Thanks," I say.

"Sure," Ever replies smiling.

We sit there in silence for a minute

"Hey, can I ask you another question?" I ask.

"Shoot," Ever says with a grin.

"Why does everything shake when you get upset?" I ask eagerly.

Ever seems to shift in discomfort.

"Since I am part of the Dimensionary, I travel from dimension to dimension. As I mentioned, I am experiencing complications. When one of the transparent people who saw me at the base comes nears me, I can feel it. I start shifting between this and my own dimension, which causes friction between the two. As a result, it shakes the earth and causes me a lot of pain," Ever explains.

"You shift between dimensions? ... Totally normal... What happens if the transparent people touch you? Will you return home?" I ask nervously.

"They cannot physically touch me, but if they walk through me then I could be sent home. However, that is not the case now," Ever replies.

"I don't understand. Why wouldn't you be able to go home?" I ask in confusion.

"I would not be sent home, because I am not whole," Ever responds.

"Not whole?" I ask even more confused now.

"You have a part of me, remember?" Ever replies touching my arm.

I look at him with a shocked and confused look. Ever sees that I'm completely lost, so he smiles, then grasps my left hand and holds it up next to his face. In sync, my arm and Ever's eyes flash in glowing white.

"Remember?" Ever repeats, as he puts my hand down.

"Oh," I respond, understanding.

Ever smiles again, and then he gets up and returns to his chair, leaving me alone on my bed and alone in my thoughts. It hits me that I'm a big reason why Ever can't get home. I have a part of him.

To distract myself from my thoughts, I move to the side of Andrew's bed and gaze down at his still face. I notice some color has returned to his cheeks. I smile in relief, knowing he's healing. I sit on the bed next to him and lift his hand in mine, then I marvel at its warmth. It's no longer cold and stiff like it was a few days ago. A small tear escapes my right eye as I finally believe Andrew will be okay. I don't know what I would do without him. He's been there for me since my dad died. After I investigate his hand, I put it down and look at his closed eyes.

"You're almost there. Keep fighting, Andrew. I'm here waiting, like you did for me," I whisper to him.

I peek over my shoulder and spot Ever smiling at me. I smile back at him and peer to Andrew again. Then I stroll back over to my bed and lie down again.

"What are you guys going to do when he wakes up?" Ever asks.

"I don't know. I guess we'll find out," I reply.

The next morning comes, and I'm sitting on my bed anxiously waiting for Andrew to wake up; Ever's watching and waiting too. A nurse has been coming in and out of the room, running tests and taking machines away that Andrew no longer needs, which is a good sign. The nurse assures me his brain is no longer swollen, and the minor hairline fractures have mostly healed. Now, we're just waiting for him to wake up.

I'm still sitting up in my bed, when I suddenly hear groaning. I snap my eyes to Ever, who is staring at me. I point to him wondering if that was him, but he shakes his head. Then I dart my eyes in Andrew's direction and notice his foot twitch under the hospital blankets. I jump up and run to his side. His eyes move but haven't opened yet. I grasp his hand tight.

"Andrew," I say quietly.

His eyebrows twitch, hinting he may have heard me.

"Andrew," I repeat.

His mouth moves and his eyes start to peek open. Finally, he opens his eyes and looks around the room, probably taking it all in, then he stares at me.

"Hey, Andrew," I greet, smiling.

"Raya," Andrew replies with a groggy voice.

Ever hears Andrew speak, so he gets up and stands at the foot of Andrew's bed. Then he smiles at me and Andrew.

"How are you feeling?" I ask Andrew.

"Like I've slept for days… Oh, and been hit by a train," Andrew replies trying to smile.

"Well that's just about right," I say with a giggle.

"Really?" Andrew asks softly.

"Yeah, you've been in a coma for a few days now," I respond, no longer laughing.

"Oh man. What happened?" Andrew asks, expressing worry.

"What's the last thing you remember?" I ask.

"Uh, I remember running towards a desk to slide under it, but I was hit with water that knocked me senseless," Andrew explains hesitantly.

"Yeah. The water carried you pretty far away from the base. When we found you, you were unconscious. Ever carried you to the ambulance, and you were taken to the hospital. The doctor said you were without oxygen for a long time, your brain was swollen, and you had minor hairline fractures in your ribs, arms, and legs. You have been in a coma, and we didn't know when you would wake up. I'm so relieved your eyes are finally open!" I reveal.

"Wow… You carried me, Ever?" Andrew asks.

Ever nods.

"Well, that's kind of embarrassing," Andrew says with a grunt.

Ever begins to laugh.

"Andrew! He saved your life!" I burst out with a giggle.

"Thank you, but still embarrassing," Andrew replies smiling.

"You are welcome, and sorry," Ever says with a chuckle.

"You guys are ridiculous," I comment trying to catch my breath after laughing.

"Anyways, I'm starving. Is there any food around here?" Andrew asks.

"Yeah, the nurse did say you should eat when you wake up. I'll go get you some food in the cafeteria, where maybe the food is better than what they might serve you here," I offer.

"Awesome," Andrew responds with a grin.

"I will join you," Ever adds.

I leave the room with Ever close behind me and see

Andrew's nurse on my way out.

"Hey, Andrew just woke up. So, we're on our way to get him some food," I inform the nurse.

"Great! I'll go check on him," the nurse replies, as she starts for Andrew's room.

Ever and I continue down the hallway towards the cafeteria. When we get there, I notice the cafeteria isn't packed with people, so thankfully the checkout line will be quick. I grab different snacks, solid and soft, not really sure what he can eat at this time. Then we stand in line to check out. As I wait behind the customer in front of me, I examine the area. I see dozens of large round tables with chairs spread around them for people's convenience to eat at. Although, they do seem to be needing a cleaning. The customer moves up in front of me to pay, but something catches my eye, so I glance over my shoulder and notice Ever's eyes dart around the room. Then he stares at something for a few seconds and quickly puts his head down.

"What's up?" I ask nudging him on the shoulder.

"Have you noticed I have only left the hospital room once, to find you, since we have been here?" Ever asks in almost a whisper.

"Yeah," I answer hesitantly.

"I have been cautious in case soldiers or law enforcement are searching for me," Ever explains.

"Oh right. Well, why are you basically hiding behind me?" I ask in concern.

"Why? Because I just spotted two officers, and they seem to be keeping a sharp look out for something," Ever replies in a whisper.

"Great," I say as I pay for Andrew's food. "Well, just keep your head down, and act like you know what you're doing," I suggest, as we start walking back towards Andrew's room.

Ever does exactly that. As we walk by, I glance at the officers speaking and sweeping their eyes over people sitting at the round tables. Ever was right. They do seem to be searching for something—or someone. Hopefully it's not Ever. Luckily, we pass by them, and they don't notice us. Eventually, we reach Andrew's room, and while I give Andrew his food, Ever shuts the door.

"Thanks," Andrew says, as he smiles at the sight of the food.

Andrew takes a big bite of his meal. Then he looks up at me and Ever, and he notices we're acting different.

"Everything okay?" Andrew asks looking at Ever.

"I am just trying to stay under the radar, since I was in military custody. Raya and I saw officers in the cafeteria keeping watch," Ever explains.

"I'm guessing they are looking for you?" Andrew asks with a mouth full of food.

"Possibly," Ever replies, as he sits down in his chair.

"So, should Raya and I say you're welcome or sorry that we got you out of that cell?" Andrew asks with a smirk.

"I am thankful you got me out," Ever says smiling.

Andrew continues to eat and chat with Ever as I sit on my bed and sift through my thoughts. With officers, and I'm sure others, searching for Ever, we need to leave this hospital as soon as possible. We can't let them take Ever again.

chapter nine
PREPARATION

Andrew's health has improved significantly since yesterday. He's practically back to his normal self, besides the fact that the nurses won't let him leave his bed. On the other hand, Ever is becoming very worried and paranoid. He won't even make eye contact with the nurses coming in and out of the room, fearing that they may recognize him and call law enforcement. I'm beginning to think we're running out of time. Earlier today, when I picked up Andrew's breakfast in the cafeteria, a TV was broadcasting the news. They showed a picture of Ever and called him extremely dangerous. They encouraged anyone who sees him to call the authorities. When I told Ever, he said that we should leave as soon as we can. Now, we're planning what we will do when Andrew is discharged.

"Where's my car?" Andrew asks.

"It was swept away, and even if we did find it, it must be totaled," I respond.

Ever gets up out of his chair and closes the door.

"Darn, I paid good money for that car," Andrew says with a bitter tone.

"What, like a hundred bucks?" I mock, laughing.

"Hey, at least I had a car," Andrew informs with a sly look.

"Okay, whatever," I say with a giggle, while crossing my arms in defeat.

Ever laughs and shakes his head.

"We'll just rent another car," I suggest.

"Yeah, but my parents would get suspicious," Andrew replies.

"So, you want to look for a decent car, that's cheap, and hope it doesn't break down on our way home," I say in a sarcastic tone.

"Well, uhh," Andrew mumbles, as he looks to Ever for some back up.

Ever gestures to show he agrees with me.

"See my point?" I ask.

"Alright! We'll rent," Andrew shouts, observing he's been beat, then he pauses. "Wait, we can't rent a car! None of us are 25 yet... Does this guy want to use his age of 546? I'm sure that will work," Andrew adds sarcastically with a smirk.

Ever rolls his eyes.

"I know we can't technically rent a car yet, but I have done my research in my time of waiting for you to wake up. I found a rental company that provides services to young renters," I say.

"You did?" Andrew asks surprised.

"Yeah…but it's going to be really expensive with all of the extra fees," I reply hesitantly.

"Ugh, great. Well, we have no other safe choice," Andrew groans.

"Okay, we'll have the rental car delivered here, then we'll stop by the hotel to pick up our bags before we head home. Does that sound good?" I ask.

"The hotel? Our stuff is probably gone or thrown out, because we didn't pay for that many nights," Andrew says in a shocked tone.

"Our stuff's there, and they extended our stay for free because of the tsunami," I explain.

"Oh ok, then that works for me," Andrew says with a nod.

"Ever?" I ask.

"That sounds good. The sooner we get out of here, the better," Ever informs.

We all agree. Then a nurse comes in to tell us that Andrew's vital signs last night and this morning were normal, so he'll be discharged tomorrow morning. The nurse orders Andrew to take it easy so his body can heal entirely.

A few hours later, Andrew falls asleep. Ever and I sit in silence.

"I think you guys should just leave without me, so you and Andrew do not get any more involved," Ever says in almost a whisper.

"Leave without you? No way!" I respond in a firm whisper.

"Raya, if you and Andrew get caught with me, you guys will be in serious trouble," Ever explains.

"Well, I'm the one who wanted to travel eight hours to bust you out. That was my choice, not yours, and you're welcome cause you're free," I whisper in annoyance.

"Raya, I know it was your choice then, but I was the one who made eye contact and spoke to you first, unlike everyone else who walked into that dreadful exhibit at the museum. I am the one who sucked you into this. I do not want to be the one who gets you in any more trouble," Ever whispers in a sorrowful tone.

I sit in silence. My hands begin to sweat as I rub them together. Ever makes a very valid point. The reason I'm here right now is because of him. If Andrew and I are seen with Ever, we could get into some major trouble. The smart thing to do is to just leave Ever…right?

No, I can't do that. He needs to get home to his family,

and in order for him to do that, he needs to become whole again. He needs me; it's my fault he's not whole, and I owe him my life. He saved me from the naval base that was crushed by a monstrous wave. The least I can do is help him find his way back home. I glance to Ever with a serious expression, and his eyes hold my gaze.

"Ever, you saved my life, and I'm the only one that can get you back to yours," I whisper in a serious tone.

Ever sits back in his chair. I can tell he's thinking about my response. Then Ever glances to me and nods slowly.

"You are my only chance, but I could never ask you to risk your life like that," Ever replies quietly.

"I know, but I want to help you. You need to get home, and Earth clearly has not treated you well," I add with a soft laugh.

"That may be true, but it has not been all bad. I found you," Ever says in his deep, warm voice, with a smile.

I begin blushing, and I smile back. Then I stare into his kind eyes, and he looks into mine. My insides suddenly feel like an ocean of soft velvet. Every anxious thought I had about Andrew, the soldier, and the tsunami melt away.

"How do you do that?" I ask in a relaxed tone.

"Remember, you absorbed some of my transmitting cells. I can feel your emotions and feelings, but I can also adjust them," Ever explains in a soothing tone.

"How do you feel my emotions?" I ask.

"Well, how do you feel when you are anxious? Your chest usually feels heavy. How do you feel when you are depressed? You feel like you are hiding behind a wall that you cannot peek around. I can lift and relax those emotions, and I can modify those feelings into something more comfortable," Ever explains.

"Why would you do that?" I ask.

"Modifying your feelings also modifies mine. It's hard to adjust my feelings on my own without your help," Ever replies.

"So, the only reason you change mine is to help your own? That's a bit selfish," I say sarcastically with a laugh.

"No," Ever answers with a laugh. "I do not like to see you quarrel with your thoughts and emotions, especially if I cause them. I simply modify them to help you," Ever continues.

"Thank you for that," I say with a smile.

Ever nods and smiles back. Then a nurse comes in.

"I just discharged Andrew, and everything has been taken care of, so you guys can leave when he wakes up in the morning," the nurse whispers.

"Thanks," Ever replies.

Then the nurse walks out. Ever glances to me, and I can tell he's thinking about something.

"What is it?" I ask.

"How are we going to make sure no one sees me, but still manage to get out of here quickly?" Ever asks, looking concerned and worried.

"In the morning, when Andrew wakes up, we'll make sure you wheel him out in a wheelchair..." I say before Ever cuts me off.

"What if they see me? I cannot just run away and leave you guys," Ever says, beginning to get worked up.

"Ever, when you push a wheelchair you have to bend down some, so no one can really see your face," I explain, trying to calm him down.

Ever nods.

"When we get to the rental car, Andrew will want to drive. Although, he probably shouldn't, since he was in a coma, but it *was* minor, and I don't want to deal with an argument," I say thinking out loud. "Anyways, I'll sit in the passenger's seat, and you'll sit in the back. The rental car's windows will be tinted, so there's no way anyone will see you. When we get to the hotel, to pick up our bags, you can wear one of Andrew's hoodies to hide your face. Once we get out of this area, we should be free from these complications," I explain, hoping to reassure Ever.

Ever sits still and seems to contemplate my plan. Then he sits back in his chair. A few seconds pass. Ever looks at me, at Andrew, then back to me and nods.

"Sounds like a good plan," Ever informs.

I smile with satisfaction, but then I unexpectedly hear a loud groan; Ever snaps his head in that direction.

"Can you guys stop talking and sleep? I know you guys love talking about me, but come on; this late at night?" Andrew asks in a groggy tone.

"Sorry," I reply laughing.

We all laugh and agree to go to sleep. As I close my eyes to fall asleep, one question swirls around in my mind. Are we going to make it out unscathed?

chapter ten
THE ESCAPE

It's dawn; the sun has barely peeked over the horizon. I see Andrew lying still and hear Ever breathing softly; they are both asleep. I slowly lift myself off my bed and walk to Ever's side. Ever is fast asleep. I don't want to disturb him, but I know that getting out early will give us a better chance of getting out unnoticed. I gently place my hand on his shoulder and begin whispering.

"Ever, we should leave soon," I say softly.

Ever moans and shifts in his chair. He peers at the early rising sun, then to me. He nods with a smile and slowly gets up. I shuffle over to Andrew's side.

"Andrew, it's time to go," I inform at a low volume.

Andrew turns over, groans, and stays asleep. Then I place my hand on his arm.

"Andrew, do you want to get arrested?" I ask jokingly.

Andrew lays there, then he finally opens his eyes and smiles.

"No," Andrew replies with a chuckle.

Eventually, Ever is ready to go, and Andrew has finally gotten up. I find Andrew's torn but clean clothes on a table, left there by a nurse.

"So, I'll be wearing this hospital smock? This isn't exactly—,"

"Covering?" Ever continues, cutting Andrew off.

Ever laughs while Andrew glares at him.

"Yes—but seriously?" Andrew asks trying to hold back a laugh.

"The only things you have are these clothes. They were cleaned for you, but they're mangled," I explain, handing him his clothes.

"Well, they're better than this smock," Andrew says and takes the clothes.

Andrew changes and Ever tidies up the room, while I walk to the cafeteria. After I pick out food, I stroll over to the checkout line. I peek around the person in front of me, and I see the officers I saw last time, but there are more men now. They are each holding a single sheet of paper. One of the officers holds the paper up, and the word "WANTED" shows above a picture of Ever. My face flushes to white, and my feet go numb in nervousness. I finally pay and walk out, but two of the officers walk up to me rapidly.

If they ask me if I've seen Ever, what should I say? I can't lie to law enforcement.

"Ma'am!" the officers shout to me.

I stop in my tracks, and my heart races uncontrollably. I slowly turn around and try to appear calm.

"Have you seen this man?" the officer asks as he points to a photo of Ever.

"Him? Oh, I saw him on TV yesterday when I was getting breakfast, but I haven't seen him since," I reply, while holding back my reflex to scream and run.

"Okay, well if you see him in person, stay away and call the authorities," the officers explain.

"Of course," I respond with a nervous smile.

I begin to shiver in fear. Suddenly I feel my arm tingle; I know Ever senses my fear and distress. My face turns hot in fright.

"Ma'am, are you sure you haven't seen him?" the officers ask with suspicious expressions.

My breathing becomes short and quick. Then my hands begin to sweat, and I continue to shiver uncontrollably. Suddenly, I hear Ever's voice in my head.

"Raya, are you okay? Why are you so fearful? Do you need help?" Ever asks in concern.

"I'm handling it, just whatever you do; do not leave the room," I reply in my head.

"Ma'am?" one of the officers ask, while moving closer to me.

"No, I haven't, sorry. I hope you find him," I say to the officers, while trying to control myself.

The officers consider my response for a second, then nod.

"Alright, thank you," they respond before they walk away.

I slowly turn back around and begin to walk back. When I'm out of the officers' sight, I sigh in relief. Finally, I make it back to the room. I rush in and slam the door behind me. I hold the door shut for a second, then I slowly turn around, where I find Andrew and Ever, who looks extremely concerned.

"What happened?" Ever asks fiercely.

I stand very still, not ready to answer. My adrenaline is high, and I am still trying to slow down my heartbeat.

"Raya?" Ever asks as he moves closer to me.

I notice Andrew on the other side of the room. He looks uneasy and steps towards me.

"After I got the food, officers came up to me asking about you. I said I saw your picture on TV, but I didn't know where you were. I think the officers could tell I was afraid, and they almost caught my bluff," I explain feeling ashamed.

Ever's face grows stiff, and I see his veins flicker with beaming white.

"Raya, you should not have gone alone! Why would you allow yourself to go through that?" Ever asks loudly and seemingly troubled.

"You don't think I wanted to, do you? But I did, because I couldn't put you at risk," I reply feeling a little livid.

Ever turns around and slowly walks away with his hands behind his head. Andrew, who finally put what happened together, steps over to us.

"What's the big deal? She figured it out," Andrew says to Ever.

Ever glares back at Andrew. Andrew locks his jaw like he's ready to lose it.

"Alright, we need to leave! The wheelchair should be outside the door, Andrew. Everyone just stick to the plan and stay calm," I inform, trying to get everyone to focus.

Andrew and Ever relax and look ready.

"Are we good?" I ask both of them.

They both nod. I leave the room to find the wheelchair. When I bring it in, Andrew just stares at it.

"Are you serious? I don't need that!" Andrew declares with an offended look.

Ever starts to chuckle behind me.

"Andrew, just sit down in the chair," I state holding back a smile.

"No way!" Andrew argues crossing his arms.

THE ESCAPE

"Andrew!" I exclaim glaring into his eyes.

"Fine! You're wheeling me out, right?" Andrew asks as he sits down in the wheelchair.

"Actually, Ever is," I reply, a little worried about Andrew's response.

"What? First, he carries me to the ambulance, and now he's pushing me in a wheelchair?" Andrew shouts and jumps up.

I step right in front of Andrew with a serious look. Then I place my hands on his shoulders and push him back down into the wheelchair.

"Andrew, I know this isn't fun for you, but we need to get out of here without getting arrested, so can you please put that attitude away and listen to me," I implore, while keeping my hands on his shoulders.

Andrew glares into my eyes, while I glare back. Finally, he rolls his eyes, crosses his arms, and slumps in the wheelchair.

"Fine," Andrew groans.

I take my hands off his shoulders and smile at Ever, feeling satisfied with myself. Ever laughs a little, puts his head down, and starts pushing Andrew's wheelchair. We walk out of the hospital room and into the long hallway. I feel my nerves kick in and I begin to feel afraid, but I keep going. My heart races; it's so loud I feel like it's echoing down the halls. I keep a sharp eye out for anyone who might get suspicious.

We continue walking down the hallways. I constantly sweep my eyes in every direction.

After minutes of walking down the halls, I see the morning daylight peek through the front doors of the hospital.

"Almost there," I say under my breath to Ever.

I glance over at Ever and wonder if he hears me, but he doesn't look over at me.

After a moment, he mumbles, "Take a look behind us."

I peek over my shoulder, and I see two officers following us, then I look at the front door exit, where I see three officers.

"They know? How?" I ask with short breaths.

"We have no idea if they know. Just act normal," Andrew whispers up to us.

We continue to walk even more cautiously. When we make it to the door, I try to seem casual and wave at the front desk attendant. The officer moves to block our path. Ever stops pushing Andrew and freezes; I do the same. Andrew stands up out of the wheelchair, and gestures to Ever to put the wheelchair away. Ever moves to put it away and the officers follow. I start to panic inside.

"Officer!" Andrew shouts to get their attention. "Please don't scare my brother, Eddy!"

The officer glances back at Andrew with a confused expression.

"I'm sorry?" the officer asks. "I just want to speak with

your brother," the officer continues.

"No, stop! He has Megalophobia!" Andrew shouts back.

"He has what?" the officer asks in a little shock.

Ever and I glance at each other trying to figure out what on earth Andrew's planning.

"Megalophobia! Fear of large objects, like this building. Why do you think he's hunched over and seems nervous? He's terrified! You really need to learn the phobias, especially at a hospital, sir," Andrew states in an offended tone.

"My apologies," the officers say, seeming a bit embarrassed and walking away.

We all stare at each other for a moment, then we exit the hospital. When we reach the rental car, Andrew hops in the driver's seat, I sit in the passenger seat, and Ever climbs into the back.

"I wasn't sure what you were planning back there, Andrew, but it worked," I say laughing and trying to calm down.

"Yeah, nice work," Ever agrees with a smile.

"How did you even come up with that?" I ask.

"From my studies, and Ever was hunched and nervous, so he fit the description," Andrew explains with a sly look.

"Yeah, okay," Ever responds with a half-smile.

I laugh, then Ever and Andrew laugh too. I pause.

"I'm not sure you should be driving, Andrew. You were in a coma for days," I add.

Andrew stares at me.

"Oh, so you're going to stop me?" Andrew asks with a cunning expression.

"I think I should," I state.

"No way. I am driving 'cause I'm fine," Andrew informs.

"Andrew, you had a head injury," I sigh.

"So? I'm good now! I know my name, and I know how many fingers someone holds up to me," Andrew explains in annoyance.

"But—," I try to say.

"Nope! I'm driving!" Andrew announces.

I shake my head while Andrew starts driving toward the hotel. I look through the back window to see if anyone is following us, but it looks like we are in the clear. A few minutes pass, and we pull into the hotel parking lot. We sit in the car quietly for a few seconds.

"So, I'll just go in and get our stuff," I suggest as I unstrap myself.

"Raya, no," Ever states in a firm tone.

"Why? I'm fine," I reply feeling a little annoyed.

"I'll go get our stuff," Andrew suggests.

"No, 'cause I'm the one who booked the rooms," I clarify.

"Oh right," Andrew replies. "Then I'll go in with you," Andrew continues.

"We shouldn't leave Ever in the car by himself. If someone

sees him, he won't have a chance to get away," I explain.

Andrew nods. I unlock my door and put my hand on the door handle.

"Raya, I do not want you going in there by yourself. You will not have any protection, and I was here with you after the tsunami. They will know you have information about me," Ever informs with a concerned expression.

"I'm fine; I'll be okay, and it'll be quick," I assure.

"Raya, Ever does have a point," Andrew adds.

"I know, but we have no other choice," I advise.

Andrew and Ever nod hesitantly. I keep my head down as I walk to the hotel and into the lobby. I am able to get to the rooms and back downstairs without anyone noticing. Once I make it back to the lobby, I go to the front desk to check out.

"Hello, I would like to check out," I say.

"Okay, what's your last name?" the woman at the desk asks.

"Fawn," I answer.

"Ah yes, Ms. Fawn. You had the two rooms, correct?" the woman asks.

"Yes, ma'am," I reply.

She clicks a few things on her computer and then says, "Okay, you are all set."

"Awesome, thank you," I respond about to turn around.

"Wait, one more thing," the woman mentions, catching

me before I walk off.

"Yes?" I answer facing her again, anxiously.

"I've been told to warn our guests about a dangerous man stalking the area, so keep an eye out," the woman says.

I nod slowly.

"Keep that in mind and have a safe trip," the woman adds smiling.

"Thank you," I sigh in relief as I quickly exit the lobby. I breathe in and out as I walk back to the car trying to calm down. Before I put our bags in the trunk, I rummage through Andrew's bag and find a hoodie for Ever.

"Here's a hoodie, Ever," I say handing the hoodie back to him as I get back into the car.

"Thanks," Ever responds as he puts it on.

"Everything go okay?" Andrew asks.

"Yeah, but we should probably get moving," I reply.

"Are you sure? You got pretty nervous in there. Are you okay?" Ever asks.

"Yeah I did…but it's all good," I respond. "Wait, did you make my arm glow?" I ask beginning to panic, hoping no one saw.

"It did, but I made sure it was very faint," Ever replies.

"Okay," I sigh, feeling relieved.

Andrew pulls out of the parking lot, and I settle in for the long drive back. As I gaze out the car window, I hope and pray that there is no trouble ahead, and we remain in the clear.

chapter eleven
PROBLEMS

Half an hour passes and so far, so good. Ever has kept his hoodie on and his head down. Although, Andrew has pointed out many cops on the side of the road, but they haven't seemed concerned with us. I'm still worried and a little bored.

"Does anyone want some of the chips and sandwiches I got from the hospital?" I ask.

"I'll have a bag of chips," Andrew replies.

"You want anything, Ever?" I ask while handing Andrew his snack.

"No, I do not eat anymore," Ever answers.

Andrew and I glance at each other with shocked and confused expressions.

"What's wrong with you?" Andrew asks with a mouth full of chips.

Ever begins to laugh.

"What do you mean you don't eat anymore, Ever?" I ask in confusion.

"Well, where I come from, people like me stop eating around the age of 500," Ever explains.

"Are you sure the place you come from isn't hell?" Andrew asks with a grin.

Ever chuckles.

"I am sure," Ever replies.

"So, you don't eat anything?" I ask.

"I do not consume any food, but I drink one liquid," Ever responds.

"What do you drink?" I ask feeling intrigued.

"I drink a violet, thick broth called cresser," Ever explains with a grin.

"That sounds disgusting," Andrew says laughing.

"Why do you drink—cresser?" I ask, trying to ignore Andrew.

"Cresser provides my body strength, healing, and overall better health," Ever replies after laughing at Andrew.

"So, is cresser made from the herb, cress?" Andrew asks.

"No, it is made from the violet lunery flower. That plant is only found at the crests of the sierras in my dimension," Ever responds grinning, as if he's thinking back to a happy memory.

"Wow," I say, while trying to imagine what Ever just explained.

"Hate to cut the conversation, but what's going on up ahead?" Andrew asks as he slows the car to a stop.

I peer out the windshield, and cars are in grid lock. No one is moving.

"Why are we all stopped?" I ask beginning to panic.

"That's what I'm wondering," Andrew states.

Ever begins to shift in his seat, he seems uneasy.

Eventually, we roll forward enough to see what the problem is. There is a line of police cars blocking all but one lane. I see officers move from car to car with flashlights. I gasp.

"Oh no. I think it's a checkpoint!" Andrew reveals.

I hear a low, dry growling noise come from Ever's throat.

"What are we going to do? We can't exactly hide Ever," I stammer with trepidation.

Fears begin to cloud my head…Andrew and I get arrested, Ever is seized and never able to get home, my life in prison…

What are we going to do? I whisper to myself, with tears welling up in my eyes.

Out of nowhere, my arm begins to tingle, and I feel a comforting hand on my shoulder. I now know that Ever senses my emotional distress. Suddenly, a feeling of peace comes over me. All of my tension melts away, my worries feel so far removed. I sigh in relief. I unexpectedly hear his voice in my head.

"Raya, just relax. Everything is going to be okay. Whatever happens will not be your fault. I will take care of it," Ever says in a soothing tone in my head.

"Okay," I whisper under my breath.

Ever takes his hand off my shoulder and sits back again.

"What's the plan?" Andrew asks nervously.

"Uhh," I mutter trying to refocus.

"Just keep driving, listen to the cops, and act like I am not here," Ever informs while situating himself in the backseat.

"What are you going to do?" I ask, concerned, as our car is next in line.

"You will see. I just ask, when the cops tell you to get out of the car, move slowly, Raya, because you may lose your breath," Ever explains while taking off his hoodie.

"What?" I ask starting to panic.

"Raya, put this on…and relax, okay? Your arm is going to shine with signs, so you need to hide it. We are all going to be fine," Ever assures, as he hands me his hoodie.

I put on the sweatshirt and pull my sleeve down until it covers my thumb. Then abruptly, I start to breathe heavily; I'm not able to get enough air in my lungs. Andrew pulls the car up to the police checkpoint. All of a sudden, I feel the sensation of scorching knives and needles in my left arm. I cling to my arm in complete agony.

"Ugh!" I blurt out, before Andrew rolls down his window.

"Hello, officer," Andrew says out his window.

"Please exit the vehicle," an officer orders.

Andrew gets out, then I do the same. As I exit, I glance to the backseat coming to discover that Ever isn't there. I look around, but there is no sign of him.

"Lift your arms and widen your legs, please," an officer commands me.

I lift my arms parallel to the ground, and I widen my legs. I notice Andrew's doing the same. The officers begin to pat us down, while others search the car. I look closely at the officer patting me down and notice he has two sleeves of tattoos. Then I peer over to my glowing arm, and I notice my hand is glowing as well, but it's not covered. I begin to shiver with fear. The officer makes his way up my body then to my left arm. Every pat on my arm is excruciating. Tears well up in my eyes. Luckily, the officer doesn't touch my hand, but he does notice it.

"Is that a three-dimensional tattoo?" the officer asks with a grin, as he pats down my other arm.

"Huh? Oh, uh yeah," I reply trying to push the pain down.

"It looks great; it really seems embedded and appears to glow," the officer compliments.

"Oh, thanks," I say feeling relieved.

Eventually, the officer leaves me to go help search the car. I glance to Andrew with a tear falling down my cheek. Then Andrew looks over to me and notices I'm upset.

"We're okay," Andrew mouths trying to calm my fear and anxiousness.

Then I clench my arm and cradle it in my other in an attempt to deal with the agonizing pain. Suddenly, I feel something ringing at the back of my mind, nervousness, but it's not mine. *Ever?* I notice that the officers are making their way to the backseat of the car. Ever must be invisible in the backseat. I am overcome with worry. My breath becomes short and quick. My vision darkens to black, and I feel nauseous. Then I start to wobble, like I'm about to fall. I stumble to the left and lean up against something, but nothing is there. Then I feel a cold hand gently clasp my glowing hand, and I experience relief.

"Ever?" I ask in a quiet groan.

"Shhh," Ever responds in his invisible state. "Breathe, Raya," Ever implores softly.

I take a few deep breaths. Gradually, my nausea fades, my vision clears, and some of my strength returns. I stand up straight again and clench Ever's invisible hand. Eventually, the officers finish searching the car. Just as the officer moves to close the backseat door, Ever's cold hold abruptly disappears. The searing pains returns, and I grab my left arm again.

"Alright, thanks for waiting. You guys are free to go," an officer says to Andrew and me.

"Thank you," Andrew replies as he gets in the car.

I slowly open the door and get in. After I close the door, I groan in excruciating pain, and I lean my head back against the headrest. Andrew starts the car and begins pulling away.

"Hold on, Raya, we're almost in the clear," Andrew says.

We're finally far enough away from the checkpoint, and Ever returns to a human-like state.

"Huhh," I sigh loudly, feeling comfortable again as my arm's going back to normal.

"I am so sorry, Raya," Ever says in a mournful tone.

"It's alright. I'm just glad we made it out okay," I respond still leaning my head up against the headrest.

"Yeah, me too," Andrew agrees.

Andrew continues driving down the highway. I peer far down the road, and I can't see any more police checkpoints. Now, I'm confident that we may actually get home unscathed, but we still have about six hours to go.

Three hours pass. I feel like the drive is never going to end. Every time a white car passes, I worry it's a police car. I shiver every time I see one, which concerns Ever, but it's just the nervous side of me over-reacting. After a while, Andrew has to pull off the highway to refill the car with gas. We pull in and Andrew gets out, while Ever and I stay inside the car.

"How much longer do we have?" Ever mumbles.

"We have like three hours left," I groan.

Ever and I sit quietly for a minute.

"I think I'm going to go inside and buy some water," I mention while unstrapping myself.

"By yourself?" Ever asks while sitting forward.

"Yes, I'm totally capable of walking inside and buying water," I reply annoyed.

Before Ever gets a word in, I close the door and begin walking to the gas station.

"Where are you going?" Andrew shouts to me.

"Getting water!" I shout back.

I stroll inside and head over to the cooler. When I see the drink I want, I try to open the door, but it won't budge. I glance up to investigate, and I realize someone's hand is holding the door shut. When I slowly turn around, I see a big man staring right at me. He has a yellow-teethed grin and an unkempt beard.

"Yes?" I ask in a shaking voice.

The man doesn't say anything. He just continues to stare at me with a suspicious smile. I try to move out of the way, but he steps closer to block my path.

"Sir, please move," I demand in a loud tone.

"Why darling?" the man asks in a scratchy voice.

My heart begins pounding, what feels like it's coming out

of my chest. I feel my arm start to tingle, but I ignore it.

"Please move," I repeat firmly, but still shaky.

The man still does not move, so I yank my arm back and throw the hardest punch I can at his face. After my blow, he stumbles backwards grabbing his nose. I run pass him towards the door, but another man stops me with the same suspicious smile. My breath becomes quick and short again. Suddenly, the front door swings open behind the man.

"Hey!" Andrew yells harshly, while shoving the other man to the side.

The man's face shifts from the suspicious smile to an ugly grin. Then he takes a swing at Andrew, and they start to fight. The other man runs over to help his buddy. I frantically look around for an employee but do not see one. Andrew continues to fight, punching and kicking harshly, but he is slowly losing. I run over and firmly shove one of the men who responds by throwing me onto the floor. The air is knocked out of me, so I lay there, slowly trying to regain my breath.

When I finally sit up again, Andrew begins to moan as he falls closer to the ground. I suddenly remember his tsunami injuries. He needs help, but there's nothing I can do. Out of nowhere, I hear roaring thunder. I look toward the front door and see Ever. His eyes are blazing white. He slams the doors open and sees Andrew on the floor. With a deep growl, Ever stomps over with no hesitation grabbing both of the men by their necks and pinning both of them to the wall. Their feet dangle two feet above the ground, and suddenly every vein in their face and arms glow in bright white. The men gasp for air and agonize in pain. The gas station begins to shake. I look back at Andrew; he is still lying on the ground. Then I glance back at Ever. He hasn't moved as he growls and glares furiously at the men. The glowing white inside the men is now beaming. I know Ever is going to kill them.

"Ever, stop!" I scream.

Then I run over to Andrew to see if he's okay.

"Ever, we need to get out of here! Please stop!" I scream again.

The shaking stops and the roaring thunder fades. Ever releases his tight hold and takes a step back, and the men fall to the ground coughing. The glowing subsides and color comes back to their skin. Ever turns around with his eyes still blazing white and his fists clenched tightly.

I help Andrew get up and make eye contact with him.

"I'm fine. I just have a few bruises," Andrew says with a soft moan.

I wrap my arms around Andrew and hug him tight.

"Thank you," I whisper.

Andrew begins to chuckle.

"Sure," Andrew whispers back. "I'll go get the car," Andrew mentions as he limps a little out the front door.

Ever's still standing enraged when I turn around. I slowly walk over to him and place my hand on his upper arm.

"Ever, everything's okay now. You can relax," I say in a soothing tone.

Ever's fists loosen slowly, and his eyes finally return back to a rich, dark blue. He lets out a sigh of relief.

"Are you alright?" Ever asks in a warm tone.

All I can do is nod in response. My face becomes hot, and I feel a small tear run down one of my cheeks. I wrap my arms around Ever's neck, and he wraps his around my waist. Then I press my head into his shoulder as I try to calm down.

"You threw a nice punch; I am impressed," Ever says with a grin.

"You saw?" I ask with a giggle into his shoulder.

"Yes! You know there is nothing wrong with asking for help," Ever adds.

"Yeah," I groan.

Ever laughs a little as he loosens his embrace.

"We should get out of here before we get in trouble," Ever suggests.

"You mean you?" I ask with a smirk, after wiping my eyes.

"Hush," Ever responds with a smile.

The men are still on the ground as we walk out of the gas station. We get into the car and Andrew drives off. Fortunately, no one's following us.

"So, did you ever get the water?" Andrew asks with a sneer.

I glare over at Andrew, and I hear Ever chuckle in the backseat.

"Oh right! I totally forgot. I guess I got distracted," I reply sarcastically.

We all laugh. Sadly, we still have hours to go. Maybe we're in the clear, maybe not, but we're making progress.

chapter twelve
QUESTIONS

After many hours of boredom and stress, Andrew finally pulls into my driveway. I notice that my mom's car is not there, so she must have already left. When I get out of the car, I glance up to the grand trees swaying in the wind, with their leaves brushing against my shoulders. I take a deep breath, and the cool wind fills my lungs. A minute passes, and I turn around to find Andrew carrying my bags to the front door, so I quickly jog over to let him in. Then I look over to Ever, while I hold the door for Andrew. He comes over and follows Andrew inside. I close the door behind us and walk into the kitchen, while Ever follows me and stands on the other side of the counter.

"You have a nice dwelling," Ever compliments.

"Dwelling?" I ask laughing.

"Well, what do you call your place then?" Ever asks with a chuckle.

"A house or a home," I reply with a smile.

Ever nods while he looks around, then Andrew joins me in the kitchen.

"I put your bags up in your room," Andrew informs.

"Alright, thanks," I respond.

"I have to go home and let my parents know I'm back, but I'll come back over afterwards," Andrew explains.

"Okay," I say with a nod.

Then Andrew leaves for his house, leaving me and Ever by ourselves.

"Are you sure you don't want anything?" I ask, while closing the refrigerator door.

"Nah," Ever replies with a hesitant laugh.

I scrutinize Ever's response, and I can tell he seems uncomfortable.

"You okay?" I ask.

"Yes. Well—I have been feeling different," Ever replies and fidgets with his hands.

"What do you mean?" I ask feeling a little troubled.

Ever walks around the counter in front of me. He grasps my left hand and cups it in his. He looks up at me with a slight smile and then looks down at my hand. I stare at him feeling confused and worried.

"Ever, what's wrong?" I ask, trying to make eye contact with him.

Ever continues looking at my hand for a few more moments, then he finally locks eyes with me.

"Raya, the reason I am not feeling the same is because I am not the same. My body is deteriorating," Ever explains with a mournful tone, then he looks back down at my hand again.

"What?" I ask in shock. "Wait, is it because you haven't had your—cresser?" I ask hesitantly.

Ever nods, but he's still staring down at my hand.

"How is your body deteriorating?" I ask beginning to quiver.

Ever looks up at me with a sorrowful expression. Then his eyes turn beaming white, and in the same instant, my arm suddenly has glowing signs rising in my skin. Ever's eyes and my arm dim, quickly brighten again, and then dim once more. Ever's eyes return back to dark blue, and the signs in my arm sink away. Then I glance to him.

"We need to find a way to get you home," I say decisively, yet downcast.

"Soon—I will be okay for now, but—" Ever mutters while squeezing my hand.

Ever lets go of my hand and walks to the back door, staring out in the backyard. I hear Andrew pull back into the driveway, and a few minutes later, he walks through the front door and into the kitchen.

"Miss me?" Andrew asks with a smile.

I giggle a little, but Ever's gaze remains fixed.

"So, Ever can't stay at my place, because my parents aren't exactly good at keeping their mouths shut," Andrew explains.

"Yeah, that's what I figured. Ever, you can stay in the guest bedroom upstairs," I suggest.

Ever nods.

"Where is it? I think I will go up there and settle in. I am drained from the long day," Ever says while turning around.

"Okay, it's upstairs across the hall," I reply.

"Thank you," Ever says as he walks away.

After Ever makes it upstairs, Andrew stares right at me.

"What?" I ask laughing.

"What's going on with you and Ever?" Andrew asks with a grin.

"What are you talking about?" I ask with a smile and beginning to blush.

"Oh, come on! You clearly like him," Andrew says laughing.

"No!" I shout.

"There's nothing wrong with liking someone! Besides, he's into you also," Andrew explains with a smirk.

"No, we're just—friends," I say still blushing.

Andrew begins laughing loudly.

"What?" I ask beginning to feel a little annoyed.

"Raya, the way you look at him, and the way he looks at you…you cannot be just friends. Oh, and he's extremely protective of you," Andrew explains with a chuckle.

"Well—you're protective of me too!" I add trying not to smile.

"Yes, but that's a different type of protective," Andrew says.

"Different type?" I ask.

"Yeah! Look, there's friendship protective, and then there's more-than-friends protective," Andrew explains.

"Okay!" I say while hiding my face in my hands.

"Raya, there's nothing wrong with liking someone," Andrew repeats as he walks over to me and pulls my hands away. "Especially when I approve," Andrew continues with a smirk.

"I'm surprised," I say smiling.

"Ha! Well, for now I approve," Andrew clarifies while walking to the counter.

"For now," I say.

"Yep, for now," Andrew repeats chuckling.

"Okay," I respond with a giggle.

Suddenly, I hear Ever walking down the stairs. I frantically look at Andrew and imitate zipping my lips together to him.

Andrew smiles and turns away, then he peers to the night sky through a window.

"Hey," Ever says while walking in the kitchen with his hands in his pockets.

"Hey, you all settled in?" I ask feeling a little awkward.

"Yes," Ever sighs, as he leans against the doorway seeming weak.

"Are you okay?" I ask beginning to feel worried.

"Yeah. Uh, I am just going to go to bed, so I can regain some of my strength," Ever replies, while backing up to go upstairs again.

"Oh ok. See you tomorrow," I mutter.

Andrew waves at him, then he walks back over to me. When he hears Ever close his door, Andrew looks confused.

"What was that about?" Andrew asks.

I fill Andrew in about Ever.

"Wow—looks like we need to find a way to get him home," Andrew replies.

I nod slowly.

"How are we going to do that?" Andrew asks.

"I honestly have no idea. One thing I know for sure is that Ever needs the rest of him back," I say and motion to my left arm.

"Yeah, how are we going to fix that?" Andrew asks.

"I don't know. I just hope I don't absorb anything else

from him," I sigh.

Andrew stares at me with a disgusted look.

"Yeah, let's hope everything is absorbed correctly," Andrew replies with a laugh.

I yawn in exhaustion.

"Alright, well you should head to bed. I'll go home; I'm exhausted too," Andrew says.

"Are you sure?" I yawn again.

"Yes," Andrew answers trying not to yawn too.

"Okay, see you probably tomorrow," I say.

"Yeah, see ya," Andrew responds as he walks out of the house.

After he drives off, I walk upstairs and get ready for bed. Before I close my bedroom door, I notice Ever's door is slightly open and inside it's completely black. I close my door and climb into bed. Eventually, my tired eyes close, and I drift into a deep sleep.

The clock runs and the stars glitter throughout the night, as I'm in deep slumber.

My heart beats double its normal rhythm, nearly beating out of my chest. The darkness abruptly turns into blinding light. A profound, hard, excruciating pain develops, but it's not mine. Then I feel dizziness, weakness, and hunger, but it's not mine either.

"Huh!" I gasp, suddenly waking from my sleep.

I look around, and it's still pitch-black outside. I glance over to my clock; it's 3:01am. What on earth was that dream? I look down at my arm, and it's beaming with signs. What, why? Is Ever doing this? I spring from my bed and open my door. The hallway has a weird tint. I glance over to Ever's door, and white light is shining through. I quietly tiptoe over to his doorway and peek inside. I find Ever lying on his back under the covers. His arms are on top of the sheets, and they're beaming with signs going up his neck and to his jaw. I notice the sheets over his chest have a slight glow, so his torso must have glowing signs also.

I push the door open a little more and stand there for a few seconds trying to decide what I should do, then Ever moans. This moan isn't like an annoyed moan, this moan is upsetting. I don't know what to do; I don't want to wake him up, because I don't know what will happen. Then I remember Ever and I can feel each other's emotions, and he can sense what causes mine. Can I find the cause of his? I push his door open but remain in the doorway. I close my eyes, and I first try to focus on my emotions. I work to find the source. After a few minutes, I find it. My fear and worry are vibrating inside of me like an earthquake. I found the sweet spot.

Then I stare at Ever and try to find the same sweet spot. I try to focus on his reactions, then his emotions, and I find it. I feel pain, fear, hunger, weakness, depression, and heartbreak.

All of these feelings are gushing out of him, but why? I look closer and closer, and I think I find it, but I can't quite "see" it. I walk towards Ever. I can almost "see" it, so I move closer to him. I gently sit next to him on the bed and silently place my hand on his, feeling a tingling sensation from his signs touching my skin; I "see" it. The source. It's a dream. I can't quite penetrate the dream, but it must be a bad one.

After a minute, I stop searching his emotions and something catches my eye. I glance at the mirror above the dresser in the bedroom, and I see myself. Suddenly, I discover my eyes are beaming white, and my entire body has glowing alien signs embedded in my skin. I gasp. Then out of the corner of my eye, I see Ever open his eyes, and they're also beaming white. I glance at him, and he notices me. He quickly sits up with a concerned expression, but I jump back, startled. Ever stares down at my glowing feet and slowly makes his way up my body until his glowing eyes lock on my glowing eyes. Ever flashes next to me and seems to study me, he looks shocked. I slowly start backing up, apprehensive, but Ever grabs my hand to stop me. As he takes my hand, a sudden rush of power and strength violently rushes through my body. My long, brown hair suddenly turns glowing, bright white, from the roots in my head to the tips of my hair. I stare at my reflection; I am shocked. Ever, with his other glowing hand, grasps my hair and examines it. Then he drops my hair and stares into my eyes.

"What have you done?" Ever asks in a concerned tone.

"I—I felt pain, so I peeked into your room. You were glowing and moaning. I thought I might be able to feel your emotions. First I found the source of my emotions, then I found yours," I explain in a shaky voice.

"How?" Ever asks in almost a whisper.

"I don't know," I reply as a tear runs down my cheek.

"How is your body capable of this?" Ever asks, while running his fingers down my arm.

I'm not sure if Ever expects an answer, because I have no earthly clue why I'm glowing like him.

"I'm sorry, Ever; I just wanted to help," I plead fearfully.

"You did—that is what I do not understand," Ever responds.

Ever takes my hand between his hands and squeezes it tight. Suddenly I feel the power and strength get sucked out of me, maybe too much. My hair returns to its brown, and the glowing signs all over my body slowly sink away. I sigh in relief. Ever stops glowing; his eyes never leave mine.

"What were you dreaming about?" I ask with concern and beginning to feel a bit dizzy.

"Nothing," Ever replies, breaking eye contact.

I suddenly feel weak. My ankles begin to bend, and my knees begin to collapse. Then my breath leaves me, and I fall, but Ever catches me before I hit the floor. I moan a bit, feeling completely drained.

"There is the human showing," Ever says with a chuckle, as he lifts me up in his arms.

I smile and giggle in response. Ever carries me to my room and lays me on my bed, then he covers me with my blankets.

"What's going on?" I ask before Ever walks out.

"You will be fine, do not worry. I will be fine too," Ever replies with a smile. "Just sleep so you can regain your strength," Ever continues.

"Thank you," I say softly.

Ever nods, then he closes the door behind him as he walks out. I turn over in my bed and close my eyes. Then I begin to think, *what was Ever's dream, and why did I glow like him?* Finally, I fall back into a deep sleep.

chapter thirteen
DISCOVERIES

The next morning arrives. I glance over at my clock, and it's 9:00am. I lay there quietly for a few minutes, and I hear some shuffling downstairs. Ever must be up. I slowly sit up in my bed. Something does not feel right. I feel—weak. My arms and legs feel like noodles. Then I remember last night. Is that why I feel like this? Well, Ever did have to carry me back to my room. Hopefully I just need to get some food in my system.

I move my legs and dangle them off the bed. I put pressure on them and I'm able to stand, but it does not come easy. I hobble over to my door and open it. Then my legs begin to wobble, and my knees begin to collapse inward.

"Oh no," I say.

I crash to the floor with a loud thud. I laugh at myself,

while lying on the floor. I sit myself up again, while continuing to laugh. Suddenly, I hear Ever darting up the stairs, and in a flash, he's standing in my doorway.

"Hey," I say laughing as I look up at his shocked face.

"Raya, are you okay?" Ever asks, squatting down next to me.

"Yeah," I answer with a smile.

"Still drained, huh? If you want, I can carry you downstairs, so you can eat," Ever offers.

"Nah, I think I'll be fine," I reply while slowly standing up again.

Ever takes a step back to give me some room, but he does not take his eyes off me. I begin to walk and feel confident for a moment, but sure enough, my legs give out again. Luckily, Ever catches me before I hit the ground, lifts me up in his arms, and grins.

"Okay, you should probably carry me downstairs," I say laughing.

"Good idea," Ever replies laughing.

Ever carries me downstairs into the kitchen and places me in a chair.

"What do you want?" Ever asks while walking over to the fridge.

"Uh, I'll have a vanilla yogurt and a banana," I reply, pointing to the yogurt.

Ever grabs the yogurt then pauses after closing the fridge door.

"What is a banana?" Ever asks with a puzzled expression.

"Oh sorry, it's that yellow thing on the counter," I reply with a smile.

"This?" Ever asks, while lifting a lemon.

"No, not that. It's that yellow bunch right there," I explain pointing to the bunch of bananas.

"Ah," Ever responds while handing me the bananas and the yogurt.

"Thanks," I say, while grabbing a spoon from a neighboring drawer.

I begin eating my breakfast, while Ever leans up against the counter and stares at me.

"What were you doing while I was asleep?" I ask.

"I came downstairs, and I was just looking at some of your family pictures," Ever replies.

"Cool! Find anything interesting?" I ask sarcastically.

"Actually, yes. Wait one second," Ever says and quickly leaves the kitchen.

After a few seconds, Ever comes back into the kitchen with a family picture of me, my mom, and my dad. He places the picture on the counter and looks at me.

"Who are they?" Ever asks as he points to my mom and dad.

"Oh, that's my mom, Alivia, and my dad, Logan. Remember, I told you about them?" I ask.

"Yes, but before I did not realize that—I knew him," Ever responds quietly.

I freeze.

"What?" I shout, while almost spitting yogurt out of my mouth.

"Your last name is Fawn, and your father's name is Logan. Logan Fawn—it makes so much sense," Ever mutters under his breath.

"Wait, hold on! Stop! You knew my dad?" I ask in disbelief.

"Yes, my parents were good friends with him," Ever replies.

"How? He lived here, he was human, and how would I not know?" I ask now feeling a little nauseous.

"Raya, your father was not human. He lived in my dimension, because he was born there. I even briefly knew his parents," Ever explains.

"He was born there? Well, now I know why I never met my grandparents… How did you know him?" I ask, still in shock.

"Logan Fawn was the leader of the Dimensionary. He was one reason why I wanted to join. He has traveled to thousands of different dimensions, but this one was always his favorite," Ever replies.

"Why was this one his favorite?" I ask.

"Well, one big reason was he fell in love with someone… your mother. I remember he returned from one of his trips acting strange. He kept on traveling back and forth more frequently until he said he was leaving and would never return. He left the Dimensionary and came here to be with your mother in this dimension—even though he knew it would inevitably kill him," Ever explains, downcast.

"Kill him? He died of cancer," I say in confusion.

"No. When you leave the Dimensionary and then go to another dimension, you are stuck there; you are not allowed to return. He no longer had access to cresser, so eventually his body gave out and deteriorated," Ever clarifies.

"Oh… How did he last so long? I knew him for nine years," I say with tears slowly filling in my eyes.

"I am not sure. He was much older than me; I believe the reason he lasted so long was because he trained his body to last as long as possible without cresser, since he has taken long trips to other dimensions," Ever replies.

As I try to comprehend everything, I slowly put my head down and push away my empty yogurt cup. This was all too much. I grab a banana from the bunch and stare at it. My dad was alien, and I had no idea—*wait that means I'm part alien!* That's the reason why I was able read Ever's mind, how I can manipulate the transmitters in my arm, and absorbed the transmitters from Ever in the first place. I slowly lift my head up and stare into Ever's dark blue eyes.

"I'm part alien," I whisper.

Ever nods slowly with a small grin.

"It makes so much more sense. I thought either you were some super human, or you had something else flowing through your veins," Ever says with a chuckle.

I can't handle all of this right now, so I begin to slide off the bar stool. Ever flashes over to my side, ready to catch me if I fall again. Luckily, when my feet hit the floor, I am firm and steady. Ever steps back to give me space, while I walk over to the stairs. Ever waits in the living room while I head upstairs to get ready for the day.

Silently, I get dressed and before I step out of my room I suddenly flashback to a memory of my dad. I remember months before he passed, he carried a strange box into my parents' bedroom. I scan my eyes around the hallway and notice that Ever is not upstairs, so I tiptoe into my parents' room. I step quietly over to my dad's closet and slowly open the door. The contents have been untouched for years. A musty smell spills from the inside, but then I smell my dad. The scent reminded me of my dad's hugs and how he held me when I was little. Tears begin swelling up in my eyes.

I bend down to search the floor of the closet, trying to find that strange box. As I search, I notice the shoes he wore to church and his favorite t-shirt folded on a shelf. I place my hand on the shirt and think back to him playing hide-and-seek with me at the park; tears are now running down my face, as I continue to search. Then I see it—the old box. I pull it out into my lap, and I open the lid.

A picture of my dad in a transparent state with other strange, transparent men catches my attention. They are standing in front of a wall with the word, "Dimensionary."

I throw the picture to the side and put my head in my hands. How can this be happening? All I did was go to a museum for a college assignment and now my life has completely turned upside down. I can't control the tears from coming. I miss my dad. I wish I could have known him for who he really was.

I take some deep breaths and wipe away my tears so I can see clearly inside the box again. Then I notice the box has signs all over the inside, similar to the ones embedded in my arm. I see pictures of my dad and mom together. I find an ultrasound picture of me in my mother's womb, and a picture of me and him at the beach. Then I discover a small, dainty necklace. It's a copper chain with a charm, a piece of glass inside of a metal ring. Inside the glass, I see a violet flower; it is very beautiful. It has a slight shimmer to it, and somehow it still looks alive. On the flower, I find white, little nectar rods with a small glow.

I place the necklace aside, and I uncover an envelope. I turn it over and see my name written on the top. Inside is a hand-written letter from my dad.

Sweet Raya,

I was hoping to have decades with you, but sadly my body could not make it. You must continue through life without me. It may be difficult, but you can make it. You are not only human, you are also a powerful being. You may feel different at times, but that is okay, because different is good. You are beautiful, smart, funny, and loving, my sweet girl. Never forget that you are abundantly worthy, and you are important. I will not be around to remind you of that now, but I hope you will always remember. That is where humans come up short here, they make themselves feel worthless and useless, but that is untrue, especially for you. I know you probably will never completely understand where I came from, and you must have many questions. The time will come, when you will know and discover it all. You have my blood, my darling. All of your answers will come soon. I love you to the ends of every dimension, my love.

-Love, Dad

I slowly put the letter down, balling in tears. My throat is all choked up. I felt like my dad was right next to me. I put the box away back in the closet with the letter inside. Then I slowly stand up again and try to stop crying.

I see the flower necklace on the floor. I bend down to pick it up and clench the necklace in my hands. Memories of my dad begin to flow through my head, like when I was little climbing trees in my backyard, so my mind flashes back to one particular day.

My dad helps me up onto a higher branch that I couldn't reach. I sit on it with my feet swinging off the edge. I run my little fingers down the bark and gently touch small moss patches along the branch. Then I peer down to my dad. I giggle happily and reach for him to hold me. He smiles with his emerald eyes glimmering with glee and pulls me down into his arms. I cling to him joyfully, and he chuckles.

"You are getting good, Raya. Your mother and I may have to get a ladder to get you down, someday," he says warmly.

I giggle.

"Well, try not to go too high. Sometimes just sitting at a tree's roots is just as nice," he adds.

"Okay," I giggle while nuzzling my nose into his shoulder.

He chuckles in response, gently pats my back, and kisses the side of my head, before we head back inside with my mom for lunch.

I blink, and the flashback disappears. I sit on the bed while tears continue to run down my hot cheeks; my arm begins to glow. Ever must feel my upsetting emotions. I slowly look up, and he is standing in the doorway. Ever walks in and sits next to me on the bed. He wraps his arm around my back and glances to me, trying to figure out why I'm upset. Then he puts his other hand in mine and slightly lifts the necklace in his fingers.

"That is a lunery flower," Ever whispers to me.

I glance over to him with a small smile, but my eyes are still letting out tears.

"Why are you crying?" Ever asks in a warm tone.

I sniffle a little and try to wipe away some of my tears.

"I found my dad's box. He left a letter for me, and I found this necklace inside the box too," I reply with a frog in my throat.

"You must miss him a lot. I am sorry I brought it up downstairs," Ever says in a sorrowful tone.

"I needed to find this," I respond.

After a minute, I stand up and walk over to the bedroom mirror. Ever stands and follows behind me. I pull my long, brown hair over to my right shoulder. I unclasp the necklace and begin lifting the necklace up to my neck, but Ever stops me. He carefully takes the necklace out of my hands, wraps it around my neck, and clasps it in the back. Then he very gently sweeps my hair behind my back again. He runs his fingers through my hair, trying to fix it, while I stare at the dainty necklace hanging on my chest. Then Ever places his hands on my upper arms and looks at me in the mirror, while I continue to stare at the necklace.

"Now you have a piece of your father," Ever says with a smile.

I shake my head, thinking about the letter my dad left for me. That's what he left for me. I think he left this for a different reason.

"It will be a piece of you," I say smiling, now looking at Ever in the mirror.

For the first time I've ever seen, Ever blushes a little, and then he chuckles softly. He begins to rub my upper arms up and down. I turn around to look at him, and he smiles back at me. He leans his head against mine and stares into my eyes, and my insides begin to feel like an ocean of velvet, just like the last time we gazed into each other's eyes. Then Ever grasps the charm on my necklace and grins.

"I will always be with you," Ever whispers in his deep, warm voice.

All of a sudden, I see white, alien-like signs rise from Ever's skin and glow from his shoulder to his fingertips. My arm glows, in sync with Ever. Then the beautiful, dainty flower glimmers with white sparkles; I gasp. When Ever smiles, the signs in both of us sink away. I look up to Ever's eyes, and he gazes into mine. Unexpectedly, I hear the front door of the house open. The sound brings me back down to earth.

"Hey! Where you at, Raya?" Andrew announces as he walks into the house, after shutting the front door I had left unlocked for him.

Ever lets out what seems like an annoyed sigh and lifts his head from mine. His hands slide down my arms then hang back to his sides. I smile at Ever, realizing Andrew annoys him.

"Are you guys upstairs? Hello!" Andrew yells up the stairwell.

Ever looks toward the doorway then back at me.

"Let's go. He'll just keep yelling," I say with a giggle.

"Clearly," Ever responds rolling his eyes.

I laugh, and he grins, then we make our way down to the kitchen, where Andrew's waiting.

"What were you guys doing upstairs?" Andrew asks with a confused expression.

"I was looking at a box my dad left," I reply.

Andrew glares at me then nods. Then he walks over to the refrigerator.

"Do you have any food? My mom needed to go to the store like two weeks ago," Andrew says.

"Yeah sure. Take what you want," I respond.

Andrew grabs something, then he sits at the kitchen table to eat. I follow and sit with him. Ever doesn't come over, he just leans up against a doorway. Then Andrew looks up at me and notices my necklace.

"Where'd you get that?" Andrew asks.

"I found it in my dad's box," I reply.

"Is that flower real? Why is it glimmering?" Andrew asks curiously.

I glance over my shoulder at Ever with a smile, and Ever smiles back at me. Then I look at Andrew again.

"Ever did that for me," I reply and absentmindedly hold onto the necklace.

"Hmm," Andrew mutters continuing to eat. "Well, did you sleep well? You seemed tired when I left last night," Andrew says.

"Yeah, I slept fine. I just felt drained," I explain with a giggle.

Then I hear Ever laugh a little behind me.

"What is going on here? What's with the giggling between you guys?" Andrew asks while leaning back in his chair and crossing his arms.

"Well, you know how I absorbed some transmitting cells from Ever, and how I can also feel Ever's emotions?" I ask.

"Yes, how could I forget? I mean the day after you discovered you can feel his emotions, we began searching for military bases," Andrew replies.

I give Andrew a summary of everything that happened last night, including my eyes and hair beaming with a white

DISCOVERIES

glow.

"Man.—Are you okay now?" Andrew asks while expressing concern.

"Yeah, I'm fine," I answer.

"How is it even possible for you to glow like that?" Andrew asks while looking at Ever.

Ever smiles and gestures towards me. Then Andrew glances to me.

"Well this morning, Ever found a picture of my dad and recognized him. My dad wasn't born here; he was born in Ever's dimension," I explain.

"Whoa, what?" Andrew shouts in shock.

I nod. Then Andrew stares at Ever, as if he is waiting for an explanation.

"It is true, and it makes sense," Ever adds with a nod.

Andrew stares back at me with a shocked expression. Then I nod with an awkward smile.

"Man, I was only gone for a few hours and this much has happened," Andrew says laughing.

"Yep," I say giggling.

Andrew sits there quietly, and it seems like he's trying to wrap his head around everything. Then he looks to Ever.

"How did Mr. Fawn last so long, and you're not?" Andrew asks.

"I believe he trained himself to go for long periods of time without cresser," Ever replies.

"I'm guessing you haven't done that," Andrew says.

Ever nods.

"I have only been part of the Dimensionary for thirty years. I have not had the time to train myself yet," Ever explains.

Andrew and I stare at each other for a few seconds in disbelief.

"Uh, thirty years sounds like more than enough time to me," I say with a laugh.

"Well, in human reality that would be about a year, so I was 18," Ever clarifies with a chuckle.

"Ah okay," Andrew and I respond.

We all laugh and continue to chat but internally I am fighting with the reality that Ever may not live if we don't find a way to get him back. I couldn't bear to see him deteriorate.

chapter fourteen
A NEW STRENGTH

The next day Andrew comes over and hangs out with us, but I'm worried. I have no idea how long Ever can last without cresser, and I'm not even sure how my dad lasted nine years. Weeks and days are one thing, but nine years? There had to be something helping him survive. Maybe my mom knows something. She must have known that my dad, her husband, was not from the Earth we know.

I walk into the living room where Andrew and Ever are watching TV and talking. Once I walk in, Ever smiles up at me, and I smile in return.

"I'm going to my room to work on my assignments. I'm really behind," I say laughing, hoping they wouldn't catch my bluff.

"Okay, I was thinking about doing that, but I decided

watching TV's better," Andrew replies with a chuckle.

I roll my eyes at Andrew. Then I glance to Ever, who's still looking at me. He nods and looks back at the TV. I leave the living room and make my way upstairs. When I get to my room, I close my door and open my laptop on my desk. Instead of opening my late assignments, I open a video chat. Then I click my mom's contact, and the video chat begins calling her. Before she answers, I glance over my shoulder at my door, making sure no one's opened it. Then I look back at my laptop when my mom answers.

"Hey!" my mom announces.

I quickly turn down my laptop's volume.

"Hey," I respond at a low volume.

"What's going on?" my mom asks with a smile.

"Well, I have something to ask you," I inform with a serious expression.

"Okay," my mom replies.

"Who was my dad, really?" I ask.

My mom's smile disappears. She puts her head down then looks back at me. Then I see her eyes lock on my necklace.

"Where did you get that?" my mom asks in a firm tone.

"In Dad's box," I reply, holding the flower charm in my fingers.

"I knew this time would come… I'm so sorry I'm not there to explain this in person. I'm sure you could use a hug.

Your dad wasn't born here, honey. He was born in another dimension."

My mom begins to explain what I already knew about the Dimensionary, cresser, and how I'm alien to this Earth too. I act shocked, so she won't get suspicious of anything.

"How did he live for so long?" I ask.

"Well, when he came back to me, he brought bottles of strange liquids. He drank one every few months. I think he had half a bottle left when he passed away," my mom explains.

"He didn't finish his last bottle?" I repeat.

My mom nods.

"Why didn't you tell me?" I ask in a sorrowful tone.

"Raya, I wanted you to have a normal life, and so did your father," my mom explains.

"Yeah, but I'm 19! I'm an adult, and I should know the history of my family, considering this is a huge part of it," I say loudly.

"Raya—we never wanted you to feel different, and we didn't know what you were capable of; I still don't," my mom confesses while looking down.

I understand what my mom's saying, but it just bothers me that I've had no idea who my dad was. I don't think she ever wanted me to find out.

"Okay, well I'm going to go," I say.

"Alright. I'm sorry, Raya," my mom responds.

I nod slowly.

"I love you, Raya," my mom says.

"Love you too," I groan.

I end the video chat and close my laptop. I stand up and walk over to a family picture of me, my mom, and my dad on my dresser. As I stand there, I glare at the picture, then I stare at myself in the mirror above it.

"My childhood has been a lie," I say aloud.

Who am I? Who are we? I clench my hands, and my knuckles turn white. Then I look back down at the picture.

"Why wasn't I told years ago? You could have said that Dad's not from here. I was never told a lick of my ancestry, not even a hint," I say angrily at the picture.

I feel anger burning and bubbling inside of me, at a level I've never felt before. Suddenly, the earth below me begins to thunder. I glance back up at the mirror in shock, and my eyes are beaming white. Then the white alien signs rise in my skin, covering my entire body, and my hair fades to white and glows. I step back in terror, as the earth continues to thunder. I can't seem to calm the rage inside of me. The secrets of my ancestry, of my dad, and the contents of his box boil inside of me. My skin becomes hot, and my fists clench harder. The thunder becomes louder and louder, but I can't stop it or calm down.

Abruptly, Ever swings my door open, and his eyes are

beaming white as well. Andrew's behind him, and his face flushes to white with fear. Ever slowly walks over to me and stares into my beaming eyes. I stare back as a growling sound builds in my throat. *What is going on?* It surprises me, but I can't stop it. Ever steps back in response and glowing signs rise from his skin over his whole body, and his hair glows in pure white. Andrew stands in the doorway like a statue with his eyes wide open. He looks like he is in complete shock. The weird thundering sound continues under us. Ever moves closer again, but more cautiously this time. The rage is like a wild fire inside of me that continues to grow. Ever slowly takes my hands, I growl again and simultaneously Ever's glow brightens. Andrew steps back and puts his arm in front of his face to block the brightness.

Suddenly, both our glows dim, and the rage burning inside of me finally cools, then the thundering silences. My signs sink away, my hair returns to its normal brown, and my eyes stop glowing. Once my signs fade away, Ever's glow dims completely also. I start breathing heavily, trying to catch my breath. Ever let's go of my hands and falls back but the wall keeps him upright. He's shaking all over and breathing heavily as well. My knees start to give, but Andrew runs over and catches me right before I fall. He carries all my weight and lays my limp body on my bed. I moan and he stares at me in complete shock. Then Andrew turns to Ever, but Ever puts his hand up, hinting to stay away. Ever slides down the wall to the floor and stays there, still breathing heavily. Andrew cautiously sits next to me on the bed.

"What—the heck—was that?" Andrew asks hesitantly, but loudly.

I groan and sit up.

"I—I didn't come up here to work on my assignments. I came up here to call my mom and ask her about my dad," I sigh.

"Why—never mind. What did she say?" Andrew asks in an upset tone.

"She basically explained my life and my family are a lie," I reply in a whisper. I hated saying the words out loud. Without warning, my eyes beam in white again, and Andrew jumps back. The anger begins boiling inside of me again.

"Raya," Ever moans.

I snap my eyes to Ever, who's slouching to the side, against the wall.

"Stop," Ever whispers.

My eyes dim and return to their normal green, and my anger calms. Then Andrew sits back down again.

"Raya, relax. Let's not destroy the earth," Andrew says nervously.

"Sorry," I respond with a slight giggle.

Eventually I start to feel normal again, so I stand up.

Andrew is still cautious, so he watches me from a short distance away. I kneel down to Ever. What did I do to him? He's breathing slowly on the floor.

"I'm so sorry, Ever. Are you okay?" I ask sorrowfully.

"Mhmm," Ever mumbles with his eyes barely open.

"Can you get up?" I ask mournfully.

Weak, Ever manages to shake his head.

"I cannot move. I used the rest of my strength to calm you…it is gone," Ever replies quietly.

My eyes swell with a sea of tears. What have I done? I let my emotions get out of control, and as a result, Ever's life was drained out of him. Ever grins and takes my hand, then he rubs it with his thumb.

"It is okay," Ever whispers with a smile.

"No, it's not," I reply beginning to cry.

Andrew squats down next to me and places his hand on my back.

What can I do? Ever is about to die right in front of me. *Think, Raya, think.* I suddenly remember what my mom said. My Dad didn't drink *all* of his cresser. We must still have it somewhere. I jump up and run out of my room straight into my dad's closet. I search everywhere, behind shelves, under boxes, but find nothing. Then I sit on the floor in defeat. I hear Ever moan in the other room, and I feel the house vibrate for a second. I lean forward with tears running down my face when I notice the wood grain under me does not match up with the rest of the floor, so I spring up, stunned. I step on it, and it creaks. I bend down and knock on that spot beneath me. It's hollow. My heart starts racing. I quickly move aside, and I find a faint seam, which reveals a small square. I squeeze my nails in between the floor and the square trying to lift it. I pull and pull with everything I can as my fingertips burn and throb. Finally, I lift the square up from the floor, revealing a hidden cubby, as I stumble backwards. I scramble back to the opening and find dusty, empty bottles, but then I find it. Laying between the empty bottles is one bottle half full of thick, shiny, dark purple broth. I grab it and run out of the room. I almost trip over my own feet as I slide next to Ever's feeble side.

"Ever, take this," I say frantically, while handing him the bottle of cresser.

Ever looks at me in shock, but he takes it from me. He opens the bottle and begins to drink the thick broth. As Ever drinks, his mouth and throat begin to change from skin color to violet. The color slowly spreads throughout the rest of his body in a pattern that looks like veins. When he finishes, the violet veins dim into glowing white, and then disappear. Ever's eyes change to blazing white, and the earth shakes loudly beneath us. Andrew and I stand back. Then Ever gets up, his eyes return to blue, and the earth quiets.

Andrew and I glance at each other, then back to Ever. Ever smiles and steps towards me. He wraps his arms around my waist and hugs me tight. I wrap my arms around his neck and press my face into his shoulder. I sigh in relief. Ever's going to last a little longer. Even though my conversation with my mom upset me, I'm glad she told me about Dad's last bottle. Her comment saved Ever's life.

I push my head into Ever's shoulder, and he squeezes me tighter.

"Thank you," Ever whispers to me.

Butterflies swirl and flutter inside of my stomach, causing me to smile widely. My arm tingles, and Ever begins to chuckle, sensing my reaction. I haven't felt this happy and calm in what seems like weeks.

"Uhh, okay! That's enough," Andrew interrupts.

Ever releases his arms, and I surrender my grip around his neck. Then I turn around to Andrew, and he has his arms crossed. I start to blush feeling embarrassed, and Andrew rolls his eyes.

"Let's go to the kitchen and get you something to eat, Raya," Andrew says laughing.

"Okay," I reply, still feeling a little embarrassed.

We all make our way to the kitchen, where I grab a snack and sit at the kitchen table with Andrew. Ever sits in the seat next to mine. Andrew peers at me then glares at Ever.

"Moving past the fact that I just about had a heart attack, can we talk about how she was capable of that? I've never seen Raya do anything like that before," Andrew says to Ever.

"I do not know. When I connected to her emotions, I found my transmitters, but I also found hers—which I never saw before. They were awfully flared, and it took every bit of me to quiet them," Ever explains with a surprised expression.

"Wait, I have transmitting cells too?" I ask in shock.

Ever nods.

"How come they've never done this before? I've been upset and angry before—but not like that," I say in confusion.

"You have always had them, they just have never been activated. In my dimension, when you are young, you are never given cresser until you come of age. When you come of age, you drink the cresser broth, and your cells are activated, which unlocks another wide range of power," Ever explains.

"So, Raya's have been activated? No—she's never had cresser—right?" Andrew asks while looking at me.

"No, I've never heard of it until you mentioned it in the car, Ever," I reply.

"Since you absorbed my transmitter cells, they are inside of you. My cells have been activated. Your cells have not been fully activated, but they are now more active, since they came in contact with mine," Ever clarifies.

"So, that could happen again?" I ask, referring back to

my rage.

"Yes—but it will not be as severe after I draw my cells back, which I will do before I return home," Ever replies.

We all sit quietly.

"Well, Raya, you better control your temper," Andrew says laughing.

"Yeah, seriously," I reply with a giggle.

chapter fifteen
CAUGHT

The past couple days have been very overwhelming, so my anxiety level is still high, today. Andrew has noticed my uneasiness, so he's brought out a boardgame from a closet in attempt to ease my mind. While we play, I notice Ever appears to be stronger and healthier, which gives me relief. We're all in the living room on the floor playing the boardgame that we've been playing most of the day. It has taken a while to teach Ever how to play, he's never played a boardgame before, but eventually he gets the hang of it. Andrew's been making fun of him. I laugh quietly to myself as Ever rolls his eyes. Then Andrew pauses and leans back against the couch behind him. Ever and I trade glances then stare at him.

"I think we should start discussing how we're going to get you back to your dimension, Ever. Especially before the cresser fades away," Andrew finally says.

I hate to hear Andrew say that, but I know Ever has to get back to his life and his family. I just don't know what I'll do without him. It seems selfish, but I can't imagine him not being here even though I've only known him for a little while. He's changed my life so much and it has been hectic, but it has also been the time of my life.

"Yes, that is probably best," Ever agrees.

"What do you know about getting back?" Andrew asks.

"First, I need to be in an area where I can feel the people from my dimension," Ever responds.

"What place would that be?" I ask.

Ever pauses. He begins rubbing his hands in his lap. Then he looks at me.

"The most activity I sensed and felt was at the—the grand building?" Ever tries to say.

"Oh, the space museum," Andrew clarifies.

"Yes," Ever answers.

"What else?" I ask.

"Second, I need to be whole. This is where you come in, Raya. Once I am whole again, I will be at full power, so I will return to my transparent state. Then I will be able to get a better idea of where I need to be, in order for one of my people to walk through me," Ever explains.

"Easy enough, right?" Andrew asks nervously.

"It should be, but we have to make sure no law enforcement see us, and you cannot be anywhere near me while I am in the process of returning to my dimension," Ever informs firmly.

"And the reason we shouldn't be near you is?" Andrew asks in curiosity.

"If you are near me, Andrew, you will surely die. Raya, if you are near me, then there is a 50/50 chance you will live. The process of returning to my dimension is very intense and harsh on a human body," Ever explains.

Andrew and I nod, showing we understand Ever's warnings. Andrew's phone rings and breaks the silence. He takes a look at it and groans.

"Hold on, it's my dad," Andrew says, as he walks out of the room and goes out the front door to the deck.

I glance to Ever, then he peers to me with a grin.

"Will it hurt?" I ask smiling.

"What? When I absorb my cells back from you?" Ever asks.

"Yeah," I reply.

"You may feel a burning sensation, but you will be okay," Ever reassures.

"Are you sure?" I ask beginning to feel nervous.

Ever smiles and stands, and he gives me a hand off the floor. Then we both sit next to each other on the couch. Ever grasps my left arm, peers into my eyes, then looks back down at my arm. His eyes begin to glow white, then mine do the same. Suddenly, glowing signs rise in the skin of my left arm. Ever hovers his hand above it, then he stares into my glowing eyes with his.

"Look," Ever says.

I look down at my arm. I discover within the embedded signs are tiny, glowing particles, and when Ever moves his hand, they follow him.

"Whoa," I utter in awe.

Ever looks up at me with a smile. Then he peers back down at my glowing arm again and intertwines his fingers in mine.

"Now look," Ever says in his warm voice.

Ever's eyes brighten. Suddenly, I feel a burning sensation in my arm and hand. I watch the tiny particles flowing into Ever's hand, and the veins in his hand begin to glow. A second passes, he adjusts his fingers, which reverses the flow. Ever's eyes and hand slowly dim, he lets go of my hand and looks back up at me. His eyes return to dark blue, and my eyes fade back to green. Then my signs sink away.

"See. It should not be that bad," Ever reassures again with a grin, referring to his small demonstration.

"Alright, I believe you," I say smiling.

Ever chuckles at my response, then he leans back on the couch.

"Ever," I say.

"Yeah," Ever answers while looking to me with a smile.

"Will you come back?" I ask. I feel kind of stupid and embarrassed asking, but I want to see him again.

"Raya, of course! You have changed my life, and I have never met someone like you before," Ever replies.

"Like what? A stupid human?" I ask giggling.

"No, definitely not. You are selfless, strong, and unique. Most humans are rude and selfish, but you are like a ray of light in this dimension—you are genuine," Ever responds as he gazes into my eyes.

I smile and look away to hide my blushing cheeks. Then I lean back on the couch next to Ever. He puts his arm around my back and pulls me closer to him. I feel butterflies return to my stomach like a storm. I glance over at his rich, dark blue eyes, and he gazes into mine.

"I am coming back, Raya," Ever says in his comforting voice.

I smile and sigh in relief. Then I lean my head against his shoulder. Ever takes my hand and weaves his fingers between mine. We sit there peacefully for a few minutes, until Andrew walks back inside, and he finds me and Ever next to each other. I sit up straight and look at Andrew.

"Why did your dad call?" I ask.

"Well, he was wondering why I haven't been working on

any assignments. I told him I'm at your house to work on them with you," Andrew explains standing in the middle of the room.

"Ah, okay," I respond.

Then Andrew glares at me then to Ever.

"Comfortable?" Andrew asks in a rude tone.

Ever growls softly and rolls his eyes. I glance to Ever then to Andrew, who is satisfied with Ever's reaction.

"I am," I reply with a smile and a laugh.

Andrew rolls his eyes, and Ever laughs.

"Can we work on some assignments, so my dad doesn't ground me?" Andrew asks.

"Sure," I answer laughing.

Andrew starts for the stairs, while I look at Ever and smile; he smiles back. I let go of his hand and stand up to follow Andrew. Ever gets up after me and follows us up the stairs. In my room, Ever sits on the foot of my bed, while Andrew and I sit at my desk and begin on our late online assignments.

A few hours pass, the stars are glimmering in the night sky, and the moon is shining through my bedroom window. Andrew and I finished most of our assignments, and we're about caught up.

"Does this look right, Raya?" Andrew asks while pointing to a citation at the end of his essay.

"Andrew, no! It should be in MLA not APA format!" I reply in annoyance.

"Seriously? Does it even matter?" Andrew shouts while leaning back in his chair in irritation.

"Yes!" I announce.

"Dude, I'm dying!" Andrew moans.

"Andrew!" I groan.

I yank the computer from him to fix his citation. After a few seconds of editing, I slide it back to him with a smirk.

"Wow, that took like five seconds. I'm exhausted," I say sarcastically.

"Ha," Andrew replies with a smug look.

I laugh at Andrew, and Ever joins. Unexpectedly, Ever freezes, and his eyes begin darting in every direction.

"Ever?" I ask in confusion.

Then Andrew turns from his computer to look back at Ever.

"Did you hear that?" Ever asks, appearing troubled.

We sit quietly for a second.

"No," I answer beginning to feel nervous.

Andrew glances to me with a concerned expression, while Ever stands up and walks over to my window. He peers down into the yard and then scans through the trees. Suddenly, his head snaps back at us with a worried look.

"What?" Andrew asks as he stands up.

"We have a problem," Ever warns.

I jump out of my chair in fear, while Ever paces over to me and Andrew.

"What is it?" I ask as I start to shiver.

Before Ever gets the chance to answer, I hear a loud slam and crunch downstairs. "Police!" is suddenly announced. I gasp, and my skin crawls in horror. Ever jumps in front of Andrew and me. Flashlight beams flicker in the stairwell and sounds of heavy stomping boots are echoing through the house. Suddenly a police SWAT team is standing in my open, bedroom doorway.

"Let me see your hands!" an officer orders harshly.

Andrew and I lift our hands in compliance, but Ever doesn't lift his. Then I discover white, glowing signs rising in his skin. Ever peeks back at me with his white, beaming eyes, then he glares back at the officers. I suddenly hear roaring thunder beneath me. I know Ever is planning something, and I don't think it's going to be pretty.

"Let me see your hands!" another officer demands.

Ever takes a step towards the officers. In response, they raise their guns and prepare to fire, and Ever growls. I can't move; I can't think, but I know I have to stop Ever. I look down at my feet, and I focus on Ever's mental thoughts. My eyes begin to glow, and I tap into his thoughts.

"Ever. Listen to them," I say to Ever in my mind.

"I do not want them to take you away," Ever responds back.

"Everything's going to be fine. I can't watch them kill you. Please, just listen," I implore.

My eyes stop glowing, and I look up. Gradually, the thundering stops, and Ever's glow dims. Then he slowly lifts his hands, and the officers charge in.

"Get on your knees!" the officers announce repeatedly.

We all kneel. The officers handcuff me and Andrew. Other officers throw Ever to the ground and handcuff him, while the rest of the SWAT team point their weapons at his head. The officers direct us out of my house and to the police vehicles. Andrew and I are put into a car, while Ever is pushed into a military grade truck. Then our car drives away. As I sit quietly in horror, I look over at Andrew who is as still as a statue, then he finally glances to me.

"What's going to happen to us?" I whisper.

"I don't know—how'd they even know we were at your house?" Andrew asks at a low volume.

"I don't know," I reply quietly.

Eventually, we arrive at a huge military facility, where we're unloaded and brought inside. Andrew and I are brought into separate rooms with a table and two chairs. The door behind me slams. I sit down alone at the table, and the cold metal sends shivers up my spine. Suddenly, a man in a suit walks in and slams a file in front of me; I bounce in my chair.

"Look at it," he orders.

I comply and slowly slide the file closer to me and open it. Inside of it are pictures. Pictures of me and Ever in the hotel lobby, in the hospital, at the gas station with Andrew, and at the museum. My hands shiver, and my feet go numb as I glance up at the man in agony.

"Raya, you know 19's pretty young to go to jail for the rest of your life. Even if you don't, you won't be able to work because nobody will want to hire someone who was hiding a terrorist," the man advises as he sits down. My heart drops as I realize my life is ruined.

"So, tell me what you know about this creature," the man informs while pointing to a picture of Ever. The photo captured the moments in the gas station when Ever pinned the two men to the wall.

"Who or what is it?" he asks.

"He's no danger to anyone," I reply.

"Oh really? Because it doesn't seem like it," the man says as he points to pictures of broken buildings and Ever's glowing arms in the foreground.

What am I supposed to say? We were planning to get him home until the police showed up.

"To answer your question, he's alien," I respond.

"An alien. So, he's from another planet?" the man asks.

"No. He's alien to us," I clarify.

The man stares at me with a confused look.

"Okay, well why is he here?" the man asks.

"He's here to study this Earth's aspects and determine the safety of its inhabitants. That's it! He was actually about to leave until you captured us," I reply firmly, as I begin to feel a little more confident.

The man continues to pry for more information, but I do not say anything else. He finally gets sick of me and cues officers to escort me to a cell. They slam and lock my cell door. Through the bars, I see Andrew in the cell across from mine.

"Andrew!" I shout.

Andrew is sitting on his bed with his head down, but when he hears me, he looks up.

"Raya! Are you okay?" Andrew asks frantically.

"No, I'm freaking out!" I reply loudly.

"Everything's going to be fine," Andrew tries to reassure me.

"Everything is fine? If you haven't noticed, we're in jail!" I snap back at him.

"Just trust me," Andrew says as a weird smile comes across his face.

chapter sixteen
THE RISK

My cell is cold, dingy, and lonely. I'm not even sure if I'm afraid anymore, or if I'm just sick in the mind. I've been sitting on my hard bed for hours, and I have a horrible headache that I can't seem to shake. I haven't heard from Ever, and Andrew's been acting really strange. He's been talking to himself and holding his hands to his head constantly. Andrew has only been locked up for a few hours, and he's already acting crazy, as if he has been here for years.

More hours pass, as I lay in the bed and stare up at the ceiling. There's really nothing else to look at. The hallway is just endless cells, and all that's in my cell is my wrinkled bed. It's stale and dry here, and I don't want to be here any longer. I need to try and communicate with Ever, but I'm worried someone might see me glow. Eventually, I sit up, because my back has already gone stiff, to see Andrew, and he's still talking to himself. He needs to snap out of it before I lose it.

"Andrew," I whisper loudly.

Andrew shakes his head, while he's still looking down at his feet and sitting on his bed.

"Andrew," I say again, commanding him to look.

Finally, he looks up at me with a sorrowful expression. I stand up and run over to my cell door.

"What's going on with you?" I ask in a concern.

"Nothing," Andrew murmurs.

"Uhh, well clearly not!" I say aloud.

"Raya, you'll understand later," Andrew responds as he looks down again.

"What are you talking about?" I ask feeling confused.

"You'll see, just relax," Andrew replies.

I sigh in anguish, then I turn around and sit back down on my bed. *This is weird. Why is Andrew like this? He's never like this.* I lay down on my old, shabby mattress and try to rest. Suddenly, my arm begins to glow, so I quickly grab my thin blanket to cover my arm. I feel nauseous and start to sweat. My eyes roll to the back of my head, and I black out. I'm in complete darkness, but I'm the only thing lit up, clearly visible. Another vision maybe.

"Ever!" I call out.

Suddenly, Ever appears right in front of me.

"Raya, were you harmed?" Ever ask as he examines me frantically.

"No, I'm fine," I reply. "Are you okay? Do you know what's going on with Andrew?" I urge.

"I am alright, and Andrew—I have been communicating with him," Ever explains.

"How?" I ask.

"I have been transmitting to him through you," Ever responds.

"Through me? Is that why I had that horrible headache?" I ask.

Ever nods slowly.

"Okay, well how are we going to get out of here?" I ask in a panic.

"That is what I communicated to Andrew. I have been trained for situations like this, and I have a method that works, but since I cannot get help from the Dimensionary—I need yours," Ever says.

"Okay, what's the plan?" I ask gaining hope.

"I am not at full strength, as you know. You have the rest of me, so I will need to borrow some of your strength along with the rest of mine that you possess," Ever explains hesitantly.

"Alright," I say nervously.

"I will only do this if you are comfortable with it," Ever informs slowly.

"Tell me the plan," I push.

Ever looks down at his feet then locks eyes with me.

"I would have to absorb a majority of your strength, leaving you with very little, just enough to keep you alive. With the power I would obtain from you, I would cast a bubble-like dome throughout the facility. This will penetrate the frontal lobe of everyone's brains, making them more susceptible to my commands. If this works, they will clear your and Andrew's records and set you free," Ever explains.

"They will clear our records and set us free, just like that? I feel like it couldn't be that easy—no offense," I say in confusion.

"It appears that way, but I have been trained to do this, and I have done it before. Trust me, everything will work out, but it will be different since I would be using you—if you want to move forward with this plan," Ever says in a sorrowful tone.

"Yes, let's do it," I respond immediately.

Ever looks down at his feet again.

"What? You and Andrew didn't want me to agree—did you?" I ask, realizing why Andrew and Ever are acting strange.

"No, we did not. It is an immense risk on your life," Ever

replies still looking down.

I stare at Ever. I know this is a big risk, but we need to get out of here. I place my hand under his chin and lift his head up, prompting him to make eye contact with me.

"It's a risk I'm willing to take," I say with a smile.

Ever gazes back into my eyes, then he takes my hand and holds it in his, sighing sorrowfully.

"I was afraid you were going to say that," Ever mumbles.

"Why?" I ask now feeling extremely confused.

Ever glances at my hand then back into my eyes.

"I will show you," Ever says hesitantly.

Suddenly, Ever's eyes begin to glow and mine do the same. I look down, and signs begin to rise all over my body. I look up at Ever and signs rise on the entirety of his body. My hair begins to change into beaming white, starting with the roots and gradually flowing down. Then Ever's hair changes and does the same. Abruptly, the darkness around us changes into light. I gasp in both fear and curiosity, and Ever clenches my hand reassuring me everything's alright. The light around us changes to a jail, similar to the one I'm in, but it's different. I realize I'm looking through Ever's eyes, and I see what he sees. He's in a cell almost like mine, and he suddenly begins to glow brighter than I've ever seen. Ever busts the door to his heavy-duty cell open. Guards charge to stop him. I suddenly see a white, bubble-like dome emanating from Ever and expanding throughout the entire building. The guards begin to ignore him and walk away, like he's not a threat or even a prisoner. Ever paces down hallway after hallway. After a few minutes, I hear horrible yelling. It's Andrew calling my name. Ever runs at a speed I can't even comprehend.

Before I know it, he's standing in front of my cell. Andrew is squeezing his cell bars tightly in his hands and is yelling my name towards my cell. Ever stares into my cell. Looking through his eyes, I see my lifeless body on the ground. My eyes are wide open and still. My skin is pale white with a hint of purple. Ever panics and rips my cell door off of its hinges. He quickly kneels beside me and starts saying my name repeatedly, but I don't move; I don't respond. He grabs my hand, but it's stiff. His eyes move rapidly around my face. My lips and cheeks have no color. Ever glances back at Andrew, and Andrew yells, "Is her heart beating?" He sounds terrified. Ever places his ear on my chest, but there's no sound; no movement; no life. Ever shakes his head, and his vision begins to fog with tears. Andrew shouts, "You killed her! This is your fault!" Ever peers back at Andrew, and Andrew is on his knees weeping. Ever looks back at my lifeless body. He slides his hands under my back and legs and pulls my limp body into his lap, where he cradles me in his arms. He pushes my head into his shoulder and lays his head on mine. The sensation of my cold forehead sends chills through Ever's body. Ever begins to sob and repeatedly says, "I am so sorry," as he hugs my body tightly.

Unexpectedly, everything disappears and fades away into complete white, nothing is seen but white. Although the feeling of Ever's emotions remain. His mournful emotions out of nowhere change to peace and happiness. Suddenly I'm in Ever's perspective again, I see what appears to be Ever opening his eyes, and I see myself sitting next to him, alive, on the bed he stayed in at my house, but my eyes are glowing, and signs have risen on my entire body. Ever quickly sits up and stares down at my feet and makes his way up my body, then makes eye contact. I jump up. He springs from his bed and grabs my hand, but then my hair suddenly changes to white and glows. Ever takes my hair in his fingers and closely investigates it then drops it. Intensely, he stares into my eyes and asks, "What have you done?"

Abruptly, the room transforms back to darkness; Ever's standing in front of me with my hand still in his. Our hair and eyes stop glowing, and our signs sink away, but the signs in my arm continue to glow. Ever stares into my green eyes with a depressed expression.

"The dream!" I gasp, realizing that was the dream he had back at my house, the night before we discovered that Ever knew my dad.

Ever nods slowly and looks down at his feet.

"That's why you don't want me to do this," I reveal hesitantly.

Ever nods again.

"Can you see the future?" I ask at a low volume.

Ever shakes his head.

"Then we'll be okay. It was just a dream," I say trying to reassure him.

Ever looks up at me again.

"What if that does happen? I cannot let that occur. You do not deserve to be put through anything like that," Ever informs firmly.

"I'm willing to take that risk, because I can handle it, and I trust you. Nothing bad will happen; I promise," I assure in a soothing tone.

"Raya, you cannot promise something like that," Ever says mournfully as he lets go of my hand and takes a step back.

"I know, but I have full confidence in myself and you. If something goes wrong, which it shouldn't, whatever you do, do not blame yourself," I say in a serious tone.

Ever stands motionless for a few seconds. His eyes glance down then return to mine.

"You really want to do this?" Ever asks.

"Yes. It's the right thing to do," I reply.

Ever sighs then walks up to me again.

"Fine—the plan will commence in the morning, so rest up," Ever advises with a slight grin.

I nod with a smile. Then Ever wraps his arms around my waist and hugs me tight, as I wrap my arms around his neck.

"I will see you soon," Ever says quietly.

"Not if I see you first," I say giggling into his shoulder.

Ever laughs and releases his grip around my waist. Then he kisses my forehead and backs away from me. The butterflies return swirling inside of me, I blush. Ever chuckles a little, then fades away.

I open my eyes and stare up at the ceiling of my cell for a few minutes. Then I sit up and glance to Andrew. He is standing in his cell staring at me.

"Ever spoke to you, right? What's the new plan?" Andrew asks, waiting to be informed.

"Same plan," I reply.

"Raya, no!" Andrew shouts in a panic.

"I'm doing it Andrew, and it's going to work," I inform him.

"You'll die!" Andrew declares in terror.

"I will not. It's going to work," I repeat, trying to reassure myself as well as Andrew.

Andrew groans then stomps back to his bed, sits down, and glares at me. I scoot back on my bed to lean up against the wall. This is a risk I have to take, and everything's going to work out fine…

chapter seventeen
EVER'S METHOD

I tossed and turned most of the night, worrying about Ever, Andrew, and myself. I may be beginning to regret my decision to move forward with Ever's plan, but I can't back out; I have to do it. I think it's about dawn, but it's hard to tell in my cell. I'm lying on my old mattress when I hear sheets shuffling across the hallway. I sit up and stare into Andrew's cell; he is tossing and turning like I was.

"Andrew," I whisper loud enough to wake him up.

Andrew sits up and glances to me.

"Yeah," Andrew mumbles.

"Can't sleep?" I ask.

"No—'cause all I see is your dead body, whenever I close my eyes," Andrew explains while rubbing his eyes.

"So, you saw Ever's dream?" I get out before I yawn.

"Yeah, that's why I don't want you to do this," Andrew replies.

"Andrew, stop worrying. I can do this," I assure.

"Raya, you don't know that!" Andrew says loudly.

"Yes, I do, and I trust Ever," I snap.

"Ever doesn't even know if you'll live! Why don't you understand that?" Andrew argues back.

"Andrew, I'm going to be fine and—and—" I try to finish, but all my strength has suddenly left me.

I collapse onto the edge of my bed and fall to the floor.

"Raya? Raya!" Andrew shouts as he jumps from his bed and runs to his cell door.

"Andrew," I mumble quietly.

I hear Andrew faintly shouting my name, but I can't move. All I can do is blink but very slowly. Andrew's yelling fades to silence. The only thing I hear is my lungs slowly filling with air, and my heart puttering inside my chest. My vision begins to fog, but I notice a white, transparent bubble stretch through my cell. Ever's method must be working.

I've been lying still on the bleak floor for what feels like an eternity. I have no feeling in my legs or torso. All I can do is watch the white, transparent bubble continue to stretch above me. I feel vibrations from running guards ripple through my body from the floor. I hear my puttering heart beat slower and slower. My weak lungs are inhaling less and less. I feel dizzy, and my vision clouds even more. Finally, I hear a warm, clear, familiar voice in my head.

"Raya, hold on. I am coming," Ever says in my thoughts.

I begin to see a bright, white light beam into my cell. It must be Ever coming. The ground releases a great vibration, and it repeats until Ever is standing over me. His white eyes are blinding with my weak vision. Ever quickly glances in Andrew's direction and then leans his head over my chest. He pauses, then he suddenly lifts his head and slides his hands under my back and legs. He lifts me from the hard floor and carries me out of my cell. I see another figure coming towards us, Andrew. Ever places me in Andrew's arms, and Andrew runs with me down the long hallway. I begin thinking, *where's Ever? Did we leave him?*

I feel fresh air touch my skin; Andrew and I must be outside. There's a strange tint in the atmosphere around us. I notice the white, transparent bubble stretching beyond the jail, farther than I can see. Andrew stops running and turns back towards the jail. He glances down at me; he's trying to tell me something, but I can't hear him. He looks back at the jail again, and I see white light reflecting on his face. Ever must be coming. All of a sudden, I feel massive vibrations, similar to thunder, and I see a beaming, white light all around us. When the light dims, Andrew looks like he's talking to someone. I think he nods, and then he turns around again.

Andrew takes me farther away from the jail. I can feel my lungs getting weaker by the second, and I worry about my heart. I feel so drained it is hard to keep my eyes open.

Andrew stops running and turns in the direction of the jail again, but something's different. Although my vision's foggy, I see shadows around us; I think we're in the woods. Suddenly, the weird tint disappears, and there's white light reflecting on Andrew's face again. Andrew gives me to the bright figure, Ever. Ever starts to run, and I think Andrew's following. The shadows around us get thicker and thicker, but Ever's glow is still bright. Ever and Andrew stop running, and I feel another pair of hands under my back and legs. I think I'm being lowered close to the ground. Ever cradles me in his lap. Through my clouded vision, I see Ever's glowing eyes and Andrew looking down at me. Ever takes my weak, motionless hand and squeezes it tight. I suddenly feel a rush of strength and life flow through my veins. My lungs inhale a gust of air, and my heart begins pumping rapidly. My vision clears, and I notice Ever's no longer glowing, and Andrew has sweat dripping down his face. I begin to moan.

"Raya," Ever says in a muffled voice.

"Come on, Raya," Andrew's voice sounds distant.

My body goes cold, and then hot, and finally feels normal again. I start to hear sounds again, like leaves rustling, birds chirping, and Ever and Andrew's heavy breathing.

"Hey," I manage to whisper to Ever and Andrew.

They both let out sighs of relief. I show a small smile, then Ever cradles me tighter in his arms and presses my head into his shoulder. I finally feel safe and happy.

Eventually, Ever loosens his tight hold on me. And then Andrew glances at Ever.

"That worked, right?" Andrew asks in a firm tone.

"Yes, better than I expected actually," Ever replies, without looking away from me.

"Good, because she's not doing that again," Andrew responds.

"Agreed," Ever says.

I slowly lift my hand and hold it in front of my face. I see my skin slowly change from pale white to my regular skin color again.

"Do you want to sit up?" Ever asks me in his deep, warm voice.

I nod. Ever gently sits me up in his lap. My back isn't strong enough to hold me up, so I slouch to Ever's shoulder and take deep breaths.

"How are you feeling?" Andrew asks.

"Uh, nauseous, dizzy, and—weak," I mumble.

Suddenly, Andrew glares at Ever.

"Did you give her *all* of her strength back?" Andrew asks firmly.

"Yes," Ever answers.

"Really, 'cause it doesn't seem like it," Andrew snaps.

"I did! Her body is trying to collect itself," Ever informs as he glares at Andrew.

"Is it? Give her more strength," Andrew demands.

"Be patient, Andrew," Ever snaps.

"Yeah, I'll be fine," I murmur, wanting Ever to preserve his strength.

"No. Raya, you need it. Ever give her more," Andrew orders again.

"No," I murmur again.

"She does not want it. I am not going to do something that she does not want," Ever says firmly to Andrew.

"You can see she needs it!" Andrew snaps.

"Andrew, stop. No, I don't," I try to say more firmly.

"She does not want it!" Ever growls.

"Oh, the alien's growling at me," Andrew mocks in a rude tone.

Ever's skin becomes as hot as fire, and he breathes deeply with rage. So, I reach my hand up to his cheek and gaze at his furious eyes.

"Ever, ignore him," I whisper.

Ever glances to me and places his hand onto mine and smiles. I look at Andrew, while Ever still gazes at me.

"Andrew, give it a rest," I say at a low volume.

"Sorry," Andrew sighs.

A half an hour passes. Feeling my body slowly regaining its strength, I'm ready to get up and move around.

"I want to get up," I say at a normal volume.

"I don't think that's a good idea," Andrew responds.

"How about you try sitting up on your own first," Ever suggests.

"Alright," I say.

Ever glances at Andrew and nods. Andrew stands up and puts his hands under my arms to lifts me from Ever's comforting lap onto the firm ground. Ever moves to kneel in front of me.

"Are you ready for me to let go?" Andrew asks me.

"Yeah," I answer while adjusting myself, so I'm on my knees.

Ever watches my every move, ready to catch me. Andrew takes his hands out from under my arms but stays alert. I feel my weight return, but I remain steady. Ever grins at my progress; I smile in response.

"Okay, I'm ready to stand up now," I say, looking up at Andrew behind me.

"Well…" Andrew says with a chuckle, while glancing to Ever.

"Are you sure?" Ever asks me.

"Yes, I want to get home," I insist giggling.

"I know, but we have time," Ever replies with a laugh.

"Just let her," Andrew says chuckling.

I glance into Ever's eyes and nod.

"Alright," Ever responds with a smile.

Ever stands up, steps closer to me, and squats down. He grasps my hands and puts them on his arms. Then he puts his hands on my waist and looks at me.

"Ready?" Ever asks.

I nod. Ever looks to Andrew, back at me, and then Ever lifts me up. I squeeze his arms tightly in my hands and adjust my footing as he raises me up. On my feet, I am slightly wobbly, but my legs are holding me up pretty well. I slowly let go of Ever's arms, and I'm still stable. Andrew comes closer behind me; in case I fall backwards. Ever stares into my eyes and releases his hold on my waist. Finally, he let's go and takes a small step back. My legs and feet are firm and steady. I begin to take small steps, and I'm okay. I feel stronger and happier now that I'm walking. Unexpectedly, my knees wobble, and I start to fall. Ever jolts to me and catches me before my knees hit the ground. He stands me up with one arm around me to hold some of my weight.

"Yeah I think that's a better idea," Andrew says laughing.

"Probably," I add with a smile. "Why'd we go into the woods?" I ask, suddenly curious why we're here.

"I told Andrew to run into the woods, just in case my

method failed. I wanted to give you a chance to recover," Ever explains.

"Okay. How far are we from home?" I ask Andrew.

"I don't think we're too far," Andrew replies.

With Ever on my side and Andrew following, we make our way out of the woods and to the road, where we walk towards home. A few military and police vehicles pass us, but they don't seem to notice us. I guess Ever's plan worked, which I'm a little surprised it did. We walk for a while before the roads look familiar to me. We continue walking for another hour, and finally I see my house in the distance. When we arrive, Ever and I walk up the steps and open my splintering front door, courtesy of the SWAT team, with Andrew behind us. We head straight for the kitchen, then Ever helps me into a bar stool at the counter. Then abruptly, my stomach starts gurgling.

"I guess someone is hungry. Yogurt?" Ever asks while laughing.

"Yes, please!" I reply.

"I second that!" Andrew announces as he slides into the bar stool next to me.

Ever hands each of us a yogurt and a spoon.

"Wow, what service," Andrew says chuckling.

"Thank you," I say as I take the yogurt from Ever. Before I could take my first bite, I let out a huge yawn.

"You're tired already?" Andrew asks, completely serious.

"Oh, I wonder why? It's not like I just had the life sucked out of me," I say sarcastically.

Ever glances away from me, but Andrew laughs at my comment.

"Well, it is kind of late in the day. I should get home, so my parents don't start calling me," Andrew says while getting up and throwing away his finished yogurt.

"They should be a little more forgiving," Ever says with a smile, hinting that he did something with his method.

"Really? Yes!" Andrew announces.

"Are you coming back tomorrow?" I ask Andrew.

"Yeah! I'll see you guys soon, and rest up, Raya," Andrew replies back at me.

"Alright," I say laughing.

Andrew waves at me and Ever, then he leaves, headed for home. After Ever hears the door close, he looks in my eyes.

"My mom's going to kill me," I say.

"Well, at least the door is the only thing that was damaged," Ever says with a cute smile.

"Yeah," I respond through a yawn after noticing the darkening sky.

"Okay, you need to rest," Ever says while coming around the counter to my chair.

"I'm fine," I assure smiling.

"Come on," Ever says with a laugh, while helping me to my feet.

"Well, what are you going to do?" I ask, while we walk up the stairs.

"I am going to go rest too—I am exhausted," Ever replies.

Before I walk into my room, I turn around to see Ever standing in the doorway to the guest bedroom.

"Go rest, and sleep well," Ever says in his deep, warm voice.

I smile and nod. I close my door and quickly change into clean clothes. I don't have enough strength for a shower tonight. I glance at myself in the mirror, and my necklace glimmers back at my reflection. I hold the flower charm in my fingers and smile. It reminds me of Ever. After a few moments, I stumble to my soft bed and curl up under the sheets. I close my eyes thinking about my day—and Ever.

chapter eighteen
HER RETURN

The sun peeks through my curtains onto my face, making my eyes slowly open from a deep sleep, I let out a big stretch and sit up. My bed is so comfy compared to the one at the jail. I start to feel dizzy, but my body adjusts as I take a deep breath. I'm not quite back to normal yet.

I hear voices downstairs; it sounds like Andrew and Ever. I climb out of bed and change into normal clothes before I head downstairs. I find Ever and Andrew in the kitchen. As I walk into the kitchen, Ever greets me with a warm smile; I smile back. He gets up from the table, walks to me, and takes my hand.

"How do you feel this morning?" Ever asks with a grin.

"Much better," I reply blushing. Every time Ever touches my hand I can't help but blush.

Suddenly, both our eyes and hair begin to glow in unison. Our alien signs rise in the skin over our entire bodies. I feel Ever's transmitters inside of me moving to my heart, head, and lungs. While Ever checks the health of my organs and strength, I glance over to Andrew, who's still at the table. He locks eyes with mine and then begins to shiver and gasps for air. Fearfully, I divert my eyes, and he stops shivering and inhales a gulp of air. I think back to the day I first met Ever at the Space Museum. When he locked eyes with me, my insides rumbled, and I couldn't breathe. I guess when my eyes glow, and I lock eyes with someone, they experience the same affect. I glance back to Ever, who's still investigating my strength. After a few more seconds, a smile grows on Ever's face again, and our glow dims away.

"You have almost completely recovered," Ever reveals.

"I'd say!" Andrew chuckles a little.

"Sorry about that," I laugh.

"Did you lock eyes with him?" Ever asks with a small chuckle.

"Yeah, on accident," I reply with a giggle.

"I don't think you did it on accident," Andrew says sarcastically.

I roll my eyes in response.

"You should not have to deal with that when I am whole again," Ever informs smiling.

"So, I'll go back to normal?" I ask.

"Not quite. You should not glow as often, but you must be careful with your reactions and emotions. I do not know what you are capable of since your cells came in contact with mine," Ever explains.

"I'm still going to have to deal with alien-Raya? The normal Raya was already too much to handle without all this," Andrew says while he throws his head back laughing.

"Hey," I respond crossing my arms against my chest.

"I am sure everyone will be fine," Ever assures with a chuckle.

"We'll see! Raya, you should eat," Andrew suggests.

I nod, while Andrew walks to the kitchen to make me breakfast. After I eat, we all walk into the living room, where Andrew sits in our comfy, recliner chair and Ever and I sit together on the couch. Ever puts his arm around me and holds my hand. I take a deep breath. Suddenly, I feel a shiver of sadness move down my spine. Ever notices my mood change and looks at me with a concerned expression.

"Well, I guess we should discuss how and when we're going to get you home," I say sorrowfully, as I peer into Ever's eyes.

Ever nods hesitantly.

"That's probably best," Andrew responds.

"I believe it should be sooner than later. I used a great

amount of my strength creating that dome, and as a result, I can feel myself growing weak," Ever explains.

"Yeah, and I think my mom will be home from her business trip in a few days too," I add.

"Well, if we do this tomorrow, I can drive us to the museum. Then you can get your transmitters back from Raya and do whatever you have to do to get home," Andrew recommends shrugging his shoulders.

"Yes, tomorrow will be best," Ever agrees.

After Andrew mentions that, I sit there quietly in my thoughts. Today's the last day I'm going to see Ever—probably for a long time. With him, I'm able to understand my strengths, but when he's gone, what am I going to do?

"Ever, are there going to be some things I should watch out for with my new strength?" I ask.

"Now that you mention it, there are a few things you should be aware of. If you begin to glow, do not touch anyone and do not lock your glowing eyes with a human," Ever warns.

"Why?" I ask in confusion.

"When you glow, that is your strength exposing itself and if that strength comes in contact with a human, it can kill them or severely injure them," Ever explains.

"Oh, wonderful!" Andrew blurts out rolling his eyes.

"The other side of it is you are part human, which means you may be able to tap into the human strength without your glow," Ever adds totally confusing me now.

"What's the difference, with and without the glow?" I ask.

"With glow, your strength is at its most active and powerful state, which the human body cannot handle. Without glow, your strength is docile and harmless... And now that I think about it, you may be able to manipulate that docile strength and use it at a more controlled level on humans," Ever explains.

"Wait, on humans? Don't give her any ideas!" Andrew advises in shock.

Ever begins to laugh at Andrew's response, while I think about what Ever just explained. Suddenly I hear a noise I've been dreading—car brakes. Andrew stares at me with a fearful expression.

"When did you say your mom was coming home?" Andrew asks hesitantly.

"Oh no," I mutter flushing white.

We all jump from our chairs and stare at each other.

"What are we going to do? I can't lie," I say fearfully.

"Well, why wouldn't I be here...I'm in the clear," Andrew comments now looking at Ever.

"She is going to notice the splintered door, so there is no use in lying about it," Ever states.

"I know, but she's not going to react well if she sees a man she doesn't know," I say beginning to panic.

Ever grabs my trembling hand and squeezes it tight. Our eyes begin to glow, and I suddenly begin to relax and focus on the issue at hand. Then our eyes dim, and Ever perks up.

"I have an idea. I will go into my invisible state, so she will not be thrown off guard, while you and Andrew explain everything. Then afterwards, I will appear again," Ever suggests.

"She's still going to freak out!" I say aloud.

"No, I will handle it," Ever responds calmly.

"Here she comes…" Andrew advises pointing to my mom as she walks past the front window.

"Just pull your sleeve down over your arm and put your left hand in your pocket to cover the glow," Ever suggests.

"Okay," I say, bracing myself for the pain to come.

Just then my mom opens the front door, and Ever quickly disappears. The searing pain in my arm starts, and I clench it in agony, while I shuffle over to my mom.

"Hey Raya and Andrew!" my mom announces when she sees us.

"Hi, Mrs. Fawn," Andrew greets, as I hug my mom with my right arm.

"So, what's going on with my door?" my mom asks, after she put her bags down.

I grab the charm on my dainty necklace and try to find an

answer, but my mom notices my twitching.

"There's something going on here," my mom says while crossing her arms.

I glance to Andrew then back at my mom. She looks upset.

"Okay. Do you remember when Andrew and I went to the Space Museum?" I ask.

My mom nods. Andrew and I begin to tell my mom about how we met a strange, unstable being at the museum. I continue to recap breaking the being out of the military base, the hospital visit, gas station confrontation, SWAT team raid, and finally how we escaped prison. I tell her that everything was cleared when the being used his method by sending commands to their thoughts making them complete the tasks in clearing our names and losing the memory of us.

My mom is in complete shock; her eyes are so wide they look like they're going to pop out of her head as she tries to comprehend the story. Andrew and I trade glances, wondering how she's going to react. Her eyes begin darting everywhere, and then she locks eyes on my necklace charm in my fingers, and finally makes eye contact with me.

While I wait for her to speak, something strange begins to occur. I want to know how she's going to react, but somehow, I already know the answer. She's experiencing anger, fear, shock, and a hint of sadness, but she hasn't said a word yet.

I gasp and look at Andrew, realizing what I've just done. Although, Andrew has no idea why I'm looking at him like that, so he glances back at my mom.

"You guys did all of that without me knowing?" my mom asks firmly, taking a deep breath. I'm proud of her for not yelling right away.

Andrew and I trade glances again.

"Do your parents know about this?" my mom directs the question to Andrew.

"Uh, they've been dealt with already," Andrew replies slowly, referring to Ever also using his method on them.

"I can't believe you would hide all of this from me," my mom says in shock.

I look down at my feet and clench my arm in agony. I don't know what hurts more, my searing arm or my mom's disappointment.

"The necklace you have, is that from your dad's closet?" my mom asks softly.

I nod slowly.

"You know more about his dimension then…" my mom continues.

"Yes, I know quite a bit," I respond while I clench my arm a little tighter. I try to hold back the tears.

"How?" my mom asks.

"The being told me a lot," I answer.

"Where is this *being* now?" my mom asks hesitantly, with a concerned yet angry look.

Andrew and I stare at each other, then back at my mom.

"Here," Andrew replies while looking down.

"Here?" my mom repeats.

"Ever, come out," I say.

Ever suddenly returns to a human state and is standing between me and Andrew. I sigh in relief from the extreme pain. Then my mom gasps and takes a step back.

"It's okay, Mom," I try to reassure her.

My mom peers at me then back at Ever.

"Hello, Alivia Fawn," Ever greets.

"How do you know my name?" my mom asks with a shiver.

"Raya told me your first name, but—I already knew your last name from Logan Fawn, your husband," Ever explains warmly.

My mom's jaw drops.

"Logan—how?" my mom asks in shock.

"I am from Logan's dimension. I knew him when I was younger, and my parents were good friends with him. He is a big reason why I joined the Dimensionary," Ever replies.

"The Dimensionary? No," my mom responds.

"Yes, and I can show you," Ever says, then glancing to me.

Ever's eyes flash to beaming white then back to his dark

blue. I somehow know exactly what he wants me to do. Ever wants me to help him show my mom how he knew my dad. Ever and I slowly step in front of my nervous mother.

"Mom, it's okay, just relax," I assure trying to calm her.

Suddenly, Ever's eyes and hair begin to glow, and signs begin to rise all over his body. My mom gasps in fear, but I grab her hand, reassuring everything's okay. Then Ever takes my other hand; suddenly, glowing signs begin to rise in my hand. They stretch up to my neck and down to my other hand, but I forcibly stop the signs from rising in the hand that's holding onto my mom. I sigh in relief that I caught my signs in time. Ever puts his head down while I stare into my mom's eyes, when I feel Ever's memories transmitting through my green eyes into my mom's. I begin to see younger Ever and his little brother running up to my dad, who's wearing a golden Dimensionary pin. I see my dad accepting Ever into the Dimensionary, with a hand shake and a smile. Another memory shows my dad returning from a dimension and acting strange. Then my dad leaves a bag on a table, and Ever searches inside the bag to find a picture of my mom. The final memory shows my dad taking off his Dimensionary pin, hugging Ever goodbye, and leaving his dimension for the very last time. When I blink, the memories disappear. I let go of my mom's hand, and Ever let's go of mine. Our glow dims, and I glance to my mom, who has tears running down her cheeks.

"Ever Winters, right?" my mom asks as she cries with a smile.

"Yes, Mrs. Fawn," Ever replies warmly.

"Logan told me a little bit about you," my mom says.

Ever, Andrew, my mom, and I sit around our kitchen table and continue to talk about what's been happening. Ever's plan worked so well, and I'm relieved that my mom has calmed down. Now, the next step is getting Ever home tomorrow, and I'm truly dreading it.

chapter nineteen
GOODBYE

Andrew went home a little bit ago. His parents had called him saying he had to be home for dinner. I'm sure they're tired of him constantly being gone. He has been through a lot, like that coma. I keep asking Andrew how he feels, but he always brushes it off. He's always done that. Since Ever has come into our lives, Andrew and I have been different with each other. I find myself turning to Ever now when I want to talk to someone. I'm not really sure why, and I don't do it on purpose. Once Ever leaves tomorrow, I guess Andrew and I will get back to our old ways.

"So, you're trying to go back tomorrow, right?" my mom asks snapping me out of my thoughts.

"Yes, that is what we are planning," Ever replies with a smile.

"That's great. Raya, are you going to help?" my mom asks.

"Yeah, I have to if Ever wants to get home. He can't get home unless he's whole again," I reply while glancing to Ever, who's smiling at me.

"Whole?" my mom asks in confusion.

"Raya absorbed a small amount of my transmitting cells. I, at the time, did not know she was like me, so when she began to glow with signs, I was shocked," Ever explains.

"Raya, you can glow by yourself? I thought that was Ever making you glow earlier," my mom says in surprise.

"Yes, I can, and that was a mixture of us, but I was the one transmitting Ever's memories to your eyes," I clarify.

My mom's staring at us in shock. Then she stares at me.

"Can you show me?" my mom asks curiously with a smile.

Ever and I smile at each other; then he nods to me, encouraging me to go for it.

"Yeah, I can show you, just don't stare directly into my eyes," I warn.

My mom agrees. I stand from the table and go to the middle of the kitchen, while Ever stands close by to monitor. I'm not really sure how I glow, but the only way that seems to make me glow is when I focus on reading my emotions, so that's what I do. First, I close my eyes, and I try to find it, the sweet spot. I discover nervousness, excitement, and sadness. Next, I open my eyes, and they're beaming in white like my hair. I have glowing, alien signs rising in my skin on my entire body. I glance to my mom, careful not to look into her eyes. My mom appears fearful but also seems intrigued. I glance back to Ever, and he's smiling in delight. I smile back and blush in response. Then I feel my emotions begin to bubble inside of me—too much emotion. My insides start to shiver with excitement, but I can't control it. Suddenly, the ground below me begins to thunder loudly. It's happening again, my emotions are too active, and I can't stop it. My mom takes a step back with caution as the ground below us continues to thunder. Thankfully, Ever flashes to my side and takes my hand. He glows completely like me and stares directly into my eyes. I can feel him calming my emotions, and an ocean of calm replaces my overly active feelings. The thundering ceases, and our glowing dims.

"Sorry," I say under my breath.

Ever smiles warmly.

"Do not apologize. This is new for you, and I am happy to help," Ever responds with a grin.

I smile and peer to my nervous mom.

"Was that supposed to happen?" my mom finally manages to ask.

"Um, not the thundering part…I'm still working on it," I reply laughing.

Ever chuckles a little, and my mom perks up.

"Your dad would be so happy to know that you're discovering your roots," my mom adds with a smile.

I didn't realize it until my mom just mentioned it, but I have unlocked the unknown strengths from my dad. I have a part of my dad that I can see, feel, and use to remind me of him. My mom smiles happily and begins to clean dishes in the sink, when I suddenly feel strange emotions in the back of my mind. A sudden wave of weakness and hunger rushes inside of me, but it's not mine. I glance over at Ever, and he seems fine, but he's hiding something. I look at him with a concerned expression, and he notices me. Ever, still holding my hand, leads me just outside of the kitchen.

"You're not well, are you?" I ask sorrowfully.

"No. Since I had to cast my dome over a great distance, and I just helped you, my body is already starting to deteriorate," Ever replies with a dreary expression.

"I'm so sorry, I shouldn't have done that," I say anxiously and looking down at my feet.

"No, you needed to do that for your mother, and besides I am leaving tomorrow. Why not waste a little strength to help you?" Ever adds with a grin.

"Thanks," I respond giggling.

"Although, I probably should go upstairs and rest so I can save enough strength for tomorrow," Ever informs.

"Okay, I'll see you tomorrow," I say.

Ever smiles and gazes his blue eyes into mine. Then he slowly let's go of my hand and turns for the stairs. After I hear him close his door, I walk back into the kitchen, where I find my mom sitting at the table. She suddenly shows a devilish smile, as I sit down across from her.

"What?" I snap.

"Oh please, you know what," mom replies nodding her head towards the stairs.

I stare at her with a confused expression.

"Ever," my mom whispers.

"Mom!" I shout a little too loudly.

"Oh, come on! I see the way you look at him, and *especially* the way he looks at you," my mom says with a smirk.

"What? You've barely seen us together, so how would you know?" I ask trying to defend myself.

"I'm your mother! Of course, I know," my mom replies giggling.

"Mom, stop, he's just upstairs," I say at a low volume.

"Oh, he can't hear me," my mom continues laughing.

"You barely know him anyway," I say while crossing my arms in my chair.

"I know him more than you think. Your father used to tell me about a young boy named Ever Winters," my mom responds with a warm smile like she was reliving a great memory.

"Yeah, what did Dad tell you about him?" I ask, feeling intrigued.

"Well, he would tell me how Ever wanted to help everyone around him. Ever would even use his free-time to play with his younger brother. When Ever got older, your dad would tell me about his interest in the Dimensionary. Ever would ask your dad questions constantly. Your father was so honored to accept Ever into the Dimensionary, because he knew Ever was going to do amazing things," my mom explains with pride. She highly respected my dad.

"Wow, I never knew that," I say softly.

My mom and I sit there quietly at the table for a few minutes. Then she stares at me with a more serious look.

"I'm still not happy that you kept all of that from me," my mom informs.

"I know—I'm sorry. I really am," I reply with a pang of guilt hitting me.

"So, because of that you're grounded. You won't be able to go anywhere "fun" for the next two weeks," my mom advises emphasizing the word fun like pretend quotation marks.

"Okay," I sigh while putting my head down.

"Now, go on to bed. You need to sleep."

"Alright, goodnight," I respond, as I get up from the table and head for the stairs.

After I walk into my room, I stare at a family picture of

my dad, my mom, and myself on my dresser. I smile and look up at my dainty, glimmering, flower necklace again in the mirror above it. This is the last piece of Ever I'll have when he's gone. The thought of that makes a tear slide down my cheek as the reality of what's about to happen tomorrow sets in. Suddenly, I feel my arm tingle, and Ever flashes in my doorway.

"Hey, are you okay? What is wrong?" Ever asks while wiping the tear from my cheek.

"Oh nothing," I reply shooing away his hand.

"Raya," Ever says quietly.

"I just don't know what I'll do when you're gone…" I say nervously.

Ever stares at me with a sorrowful but warm look, then he smiles.

"Raya, if it makes you feel any better—I do not know what I will do without you either. I am coming back, Raya—for you," Ever says now holding my hand.

My heart skips a beat. The butterflies return in my stomach, and I'm overwhelmed with relief knowing that he wants to come back for me. I wrap my arms around his neck and press my face into his shoulder, while he wraps his arms around my waist and hugs me tight.

"Be happy and live your life while I am gone. I do not want you to be upset, but I assure you I will come back," Ever assures in his deep, warm voice.

"Okay—same goes for you too," I can't help but giggle.

Ever begins to chuckle as he releases his tight hug.

"I will see you tomorrow, Raya. Sleep well," Ever says with a grin.

"Thanks, you too," I reply back, smiling.

Ever grins then leaves for his room. Once he leaves, I close my door, change, and climb into bed for the night.

The moon comes and goes and then the sun rises on the day I've been dreading. The moment I open my eyes, I have a terrible feeling in my stomach. I know what's about to come. I crawl out of bed, prepare for the day, and begrudgingly walk downstairs. No one's awake yet, so I eat breakfast by myself. Afterwards, I step outside into the backyard to get some fresh air. I stare up at the towering trees above me and I feel the morning breeze sift through my long hair. Today's going to be hard, but it has to be done. I continue to try and get my mind off of what's to come and focus on the nature around me. Then I hear a door open behind me, and I feel familiar hands come around my waist from behind. A smile grows on my face, and I turn around. Ever takes his hands off of my waist and grasps my hands in his with a smile.

"You slept in," I say smiling.

"You woke up early," Ever responds with a chuckle.

We stand in silence and listen to leaves shuffling in the

trees for a moment.

"I hope you are not too sad. The last thing I want to see of you is your beautiful smile," Ever says warmly.

I smile in response and peer into his eyes.

"I'll do my absolute best," I reply.

Ever grins and nods with satisfaction.

"How long do you think you'll be gone?" I ask hoping he'll say like a week.

"I do not know. I have to return and brief the Dimensionary on what information I have gathered and seen. Then I have to see my family and refill on cresser. I will request another assignment, so I can be sent here again, but I do not know how long that will take. Although, I assure you I will try and make it as fast as possible," Ever explains.

I nod, showing I understand. Then I suddenly hear footsteps behind Ever. Ever snaps his head around in response to see who it is.

"Relax, it's just me," Andrew reveals while laughing.

"Hey, Andrew," I greet.

"So, let's get this show on the road," Andrew says.

We walk to Andrew's car and climb in. I sit in the passenger's seat, and Ever sits in the back. Andrew pulls out of the driveway and heads towards the Space Museum. After a few minutes of driving, Andrew looks up into his rear view mirror at Ever.

"During the process of you returning to your dimension, is there going to be a lot of noise and shaking?" Andrew asks.

"Yes, there will be a lot of both, so as soon as I am gone, leave so no one gets suspicious," Ever explains.

"Alright," Andrew responds.

"Ever, after you absorb your cells back from me, will I feel different?" I ask.

"I am not 100% sure, but you may feel slightly weaker, and you may experience a small amount of withdrawal. Andrew, you may want to monitor her afterwards, just in case," Ever advises.

"Yeah, I'll do that," Andrew says.

"Okay," I mutter.

Twenty minutes pass, and we finally make it to the Space Museum. The once magnificent Space Museum that I loved is now in crumbling pieces. There's a long fence around the perimeter of the building to prevent people from entering the unsafe area. Andrew pulls to the side of the fence and parks the car. We get out of the car and climb over the fence. We stand in front of the damaged museum while Ever looks around.

"Do you sense any of your people here?" I ask.

"Not yet. I will not know until I am out of this human state," Ever replies.

Suddenly, Ever's eyes begin to beam white, and he

changes to his transparent state. I feel pressure inside of me, but I'm not in pain yet and I'm not glowing. Then Ever's eyes dim and he returns to a human state.

"They are here," Ever informs us in a serious tone.

"Okay, let's get this over with," Andrew sighs.

I'm suddenly afraid and completely heartbroken. My heart's racing. It's time; Ever has to leave. I don't want him to, but it has to be this way. Ever shakes Andrew's hand, thanking him for all of his help and hopes to see him soon. Then Ever stops in front of me and senses my emotional distress. He expresses a sorrowful smile and takes my hands with his.

"I am coming back," Ever says in his deep, warm voice.

Suddenly, our hair and eyes begin to glow in sync, and our glowing signs rise in our bodies. Ever stares into my beaming eyes with his and smiles. Andrew takes a few steps back and shields his eyes with one of his arms to protect them from our glow. Out of nowhere, my sorrowful emotions change to peaceful ones and I smile in relief.

"There is that beautiful smile I love," Ever grins from ear to ear.

Ever wraps me in his arms and hugs me tighter than he ever has, while I wrap mine around him. We stand there for a while, then Ever places his forehead against mine. Ever slowly kisses my cheek and smiles. Then he releases his hug and takes my hands. Ever's beaming eyes gaze into mine, and

I smile.

"Are you ready?" Ever asks.

"Yes," I whisper.

I feel a sudden burning sensation throughout my entire body, and the ground begins roaring underneath us. Ever gradually becomes brighter and brighter, while I begin to dim. Eventually, my glow dims completely. Ever lets go of my hands, and I feel a sense of emptiness inside of me without that piece of him. Andrew runs up behind me and pulls me back a few feet. Ever returns to his transparent state, but he continues to glow brighter than I've ever seen. He looks around with his shining eyes, and he seems even more powerful now. Then he peers towards my direction.

"Goodbye, Raya," Ever says.

"Bye, Ever," I whisper with tears starting to run down my cheeks.

Ever turns around and starts walking away. The further away he gets, the brighter he becomes. Suddenly, Ever's beaming light stretches all around him, and the earth shakes with a thunderous roar. Finally with a roaring, snapping sound, he's gone. I gasp as the flash and thunder disappear with Ever. Andrew and I stand there silently for a moment as we listen to the thunder echo in the distance. Then Andrew slowly glances to my shocked, pale face.

"Let's get going," Andrew says softly.

I'm frozen in sorrow and weakness, so Andrew puts his arm around my back and leads me back to the car. Once we reach the fence, Andrew gives me a boost over, before he climbs over after me. Then we get into the car and drive away. As we pass the crumbling museum, I stare out the car window in misery.

"He's gone," I whisper.

chapter twenty
BELOVED

I'm silent and paralyzed from heartache the entire drive home. Andrew tries to cheer me up, but it's no use. When we pull back into my driveway, I still feel weak to move so Andrew lifts me up and walks with me into my house. Andrew and I sit down in my living room on the couch, but all I want to do is be alone. I know I shouldn't be this upset, but I can't seem to get past it.

"Raya, I know it hurts but—Ever wouldn't want you to be like this…" Andrew says sorrowfully.

I sit there quietly.

"I know," I mumble with a frog in my throat.

Andrew glances to me and does not seem satisfied with my response, so he rests his hand on my shoulder. My eyes flood with tears while my face grows hot. Andrew notices and puts his arm around my shoulders. I can no longer hold back my tears, and they come pouring out. I cover my face with my hands and Andrew leans my head against his shoulder. Andrew stays with me until I can't cry anymore.

The days have been very slow. Andrew tries to come over, but I haven't been very social. It's been three days since Ever left, and my heart still hurts. I'm back to my normal strength, but I haven't been talking. As I sit at my desk in my room, trying to finish up some homework assignments, my hand naturally goes to my necklace. I play with the flower charm in my fingers as I stare at my computer screen. I have no motivation to do anything else these days. My door creaks, snapping me out of my trance. I hear someone walk up behind me, but I don't turn around.

"Raya, why don't you invite Andrew over so you can have some company?" my mom asks resting her hands on my shoulders.

I don't respond.

"Okay, well I'll be downstairs if you need anything," my mom sighs and I hear her walking away.

I turn around.

"Mom," I say.

"Yes?" my mom replies stopping in my doorway.

"What did you do when Dad left for his home?" I ask.

My mom walks to my bed and sits down, then she looks

at me.

"So, when your dad and I first met, he was on a three-month assignment. After those three months, he left for his home and then came back regularly to see me and complete requested assignments. Then one time he told me he was going to be gone for a long time on another assignment back at his home and didn't know when he would return, although he promised he would. When he left, I was upset and lonely for a while, but eventually I escaped my shell. I started living my life and feeling happy again. I'm not going to lie, it took a while, but I knew your father was coming back. In the meantime, I enjoyed the little things and had fun," my mom explains warmly.

"Okay," I respond with a nod.

"Take your time, Raya. I know you love Ever, and he loves you, so it's going to take time," my mom says while getting up from my bed.

"Love?" I ask looking at her with a confused expression.

"Raya, you've sacrificed your life for him, and he's done the same thing for you, multiple times. That's love, whether you want to admit it or not," my mom chuckles a little as she walks out of my room.

I sit at my desk pondering what my mom just said in disbelief. In my heart I knows she's right. Ever must love me if he's doing everything he can to protect me and promising to return. I must love him since I'm willing to sacrifice my life for him. I get up from my desk and tiptoe to my mom's room. I open my dad's closet and find his box. I sift through it and take out the letter he left for me, but then I find something I didn't notice before. It's a picture of my dad accepting Ever into the Dimensionary. I pick it up and stare at it with tears swelling up in my eyes. I can't help but smile. I take both the photo and letter back to my room. I place my dad's letter next to the family picture on my dresser and then I place the picture of my dad and Ever against my dresser mirror. I smile at the photo and my hand goes to my necklace charm.

I suddenly remember what Ever told me, "Be happy and live your life while I am gone. I do not want you to be upset, but I assure you, I will come back." I smile even more while a tear runs down my cheek.

"That's what I'll do," I say out loud.

I'm going to be happy and live my life, and I know one person who can make that happen. I run over to my phone and call Andrew; he's been dying for me to call. Andrew picks up on the first ring and I ask him if he wants to come over. He says he will come right over. Once the conversation ends, I hang up and smile again at the picture of Ever on my dresser. He told me to be happy and live my life; I will do my best to follow through.

Six months ago… That's how long it's been since Ever

left in a flash. In those six months, I have been living my life happily. Andrew and I have basically seen each other every day to go hiking, hang out, and finish up homework at each other's houses. We're all caught up on our college work and close to graduating. My mom's excited about that, and she's excited to know that my heart's healing since Ever left. Shortly after he left, the rebuilding of the Space Museum began. That place still intrigues me to this day, so Andrew and I visit it from time to time and even tour the limited time exhibits. Although, they have not been as interesting as the first time we went and met Ever.

The last thing that I felt of Ever was the earth shake beneath me; then he was gone. It's amazing how something so close, but so far, can hurt so badly when it's gone. Ever still has not returned, but I haven't given up hope. I know he will come back, so I'm focusing on enjoying my life.

I applied for a job at the new, rebuilt Space Museum, and I just found out I was accepted. I grab my phone and call Andrew.

"Hello?" Andrew answers.

"Guess what?" I ask with excitement.

"What?" Andrew asks laughing

"I got it!" I announce.

"Nice! I knew they would accept you! I'll be over in a minute, so we can celebrate!" Andrew shouts.

"Sounds awesome!" I reply laughing.

A few minutes later, I hear Andrew pull up in his new car in the driveway. He finally bought a new one since his old car was totaled by the tsunami; he's very proud of it, especially since its red. I run downstairs to our new, front door.

"Bye, Mom! I'm going with Andrew!" I shout so she can hear me from the living room.

"Bye, be safe!" my mom shouts back.

I run outside and jump into Andrew's car, and then he drives away.

"So, when do you start?" Andrew asks.

"Next week," I reply.

"Did they assign you to anything specific?" Andrew asks.

"Yeah actually. They want me to work in the limited time exhibits and help the guests," I explain with a laugh.

"Coincidence?" Andrew asks with a chuckle.

"Yes," I answer laughing.

"That'll be fun," Andrew says.

"Yeah, I think so," I say nodding.

After about ten minutes, we pull into an ice cream parlor in town. It's a small, old place, but its large front windows and antique lights on the inside make it feel big and bright. We came at an off time so there aren't that many people here. Andrew buys us our favorite ice cream, chocolate. Though we like the same ice cream, we like completely different toppings.

I've never been a fan of many toppings, so I have nothing, but Andrew always covers his with nuts, fruit, and sprinkles. Then we sit down to eat at one of the vintage, light blue tables inside.

"Are you still doing okay?" Andrew asks with a mouth full of ice cream.

"With what?" I ask.

"You know, Ever," Andrew says softly, like he's almost afraid to ask.

"Oh, yeah. I'm fine," I reply twirling my spoon in my cup.

"It's been six months. When do you think he'll be back?" Andrew asks with a worried expression.

"I don't know, but I'm just going to be patient. He'll be back sooner or later I suppose," I respond with a smile.

"That's good," Andrew says while looking down.

"You okay?" I ask with a laugh.

"I just really miss Ever," Andrew mutters while covering his face with his hand.

I stare at Andrew in shock. I can't make eye contact with him because he's covering his face. Out of nowhere, I feel warmth growing in my eyes, and I sense mischief, humor, and a bit of excitement.

"Knock it off!" I shout with a laugh, once I figure out what he's doing.

Andrew begins to laugh hysterically and looks up at me

again, but then he freezes.

"Raya, your eyes are glowing," Andrew informs in shock.

"What?" I ask quickly while looking down and closing my eyes.

I slowly open my eyes and look up again.

"Did they stop?" I ask hesitantly.

"Yeah," Andrew answers laughing.

"I haven't done that in a while," I say, surprised.

"No, you haven't. That's how you caught me, right?" Andrew asks with a laugh.

"Yes, actually," I reply giggling.

"I'm never going to be safe," Andrew says sarcastically.

"I haven't done that in a while, so relax," I say with a laugh.

I catch Andrew staring at my necklace as we finish up our ice cream.

"Have you ever taken that necklace off?" Andrew asks.

"Nope. Never have, never will," I respond with a smile as I absentmindedly hold the charm in my fingers.

"He's coming back Raya; I know he is. Especially after what he told me," Andrew adds with a smile.

"What did he say?" I ask quickly.

"Yeah, when he shook my hand to say bye, he told me to take care of his 'beloved Raya,'" Andrew replies. I naturally begin to blush. "I was kind of disgusted when he told me that, but I was like, 'uh, duh, why wouldn't I?'" Andrew continues rolling his eyes.

"Andrew!" I shout as I begin to laugh.

"Just saying," Andrew says as he gets up from his chair.

We leave the ice cream parlor and drive away in Andrew's car. As I look out the window, I smile and think about what Ever told Andrew, "Take care of my beloved Raya." This thought makes me blush; I laugh to myself. Ever will return, just like my dad came back for my mom. In the meantime, I'm going to enjoy my life, like how Ever wants and how I should.

Time is a funny thing. It seems like only yesterday Ever left for his home with thunder right before my eyes, but that was about a year ago. Throughout that year, I've been working at the Space Museum, so I'm here early most mornings, but today my manager wanted me to open up the place. As I walk towards the entrance, the cool, early morning breeze flicks my hair. I grab the keys from my pocket to unlock the door. As I slide the key into the door lock, I freeze in complete shock. My hand has white, glowing alien signs rising in my left hand and arm. My arm hasn't glowed like this since—Ever...

※ *EVER* ※

acknowledgments

Thank you:

... Schatz family: Dave, Angie, Nate, and Jon for listening to my rough draft and encouraging me to publish my story. You all are the reason why I pursued this path and I am immensely grateful for your love, encouragement, prayers, and long-lasting friendship.

... Payton Stepkoski for your advice and creativity. You have provided new points of view and visualizations through your incredible, God-given gift. You sketched out my rough vision into reality, and now, it is my cover! I am so thankful that you are my sister and the best ambassador I could ask for!

... Jim and Amie Stepkoski for your love and support throughout this entire process. I could never ask for better parents; I am truly blessed to have you.

... Tom Goodlet for your special offer that made all of this possible. Thanks for your encouragement, advice, and guidance to help me discover my potential.

... Jodi Costa for your amazing work putting this book together. The moment I saw the first formatted version you created—I was blown away! You are so talented, and I am so thankful that you are a part of my team.

… Sarah Williams, Jessica Conley, and Amie Stepkoski for your guidance with grammar and story development. You turned a good story into a great one!

… Chelsea Dennard, Nicole Quick, Angela Dennison, Jane Sutton, Katie Griffith, Bethany Eckert, Tessa Dury, Hannah Connor, Eliana McIntire, and Payton Stepkoski for supporting, encouraging, sharing, liking, commenting, and re-posting. I am blessed to have an amazing team and wonderful friendships!

… Angie Schatz and Katie Griffith for spreading the word and giving advice, encouragement, and love.

… Laura Sherman and Jon Marshall for taking promoting to the stars! I am so thankful for your support.

… Adrian Traurig for your incredible artistic eye with photography and design. You made my black and white ideas into a vivid reality!

… Andrew and Kaylyn Frazier for nailing the silhouettes of Ever and Raya. I am blessed to have my awesome youth pastor and good friend help me accomplish this dream that I will remember forever.

… Griffin Gilstrap, Stephen and Rachel Law, Dr. Raul Serrano, Jack Smith, Wesley Dennard, Eric Turner, Vivian and Evana Foisy, Sarah Ludwick, the whole Stepkoski family, extended family, and many loving friends for your support, prayers, encouragement, laughs, and guidance.

… Harborside Christian Church for building my faith and reliance on my Creator. Thanks for helping me discover my God-given gifts.

… My many professors at St. Petersburg College for helping me discover my passion. Thanks to everyone who supported me, including Rana Wilson, Frederick Oppliger, Roger Watts, and Roxana Levin.

Made in United States
North Haven, CT
19 March 2022